THE SWISS FAMILY ROBINSON

Climbing the palm trees

The Swiss Family Robinson

JOHANN RUDOLF WYSS

WORDSWORTH CLASSICS

For my husband
ANTHONY JOHN RANSON
with love from your wife, the publisher.
Eternally grateful for your
unconditional love.

Readers who are interested in other titles from
Wordsworth Editions are invited to visit our website at
www.wordsworth-editions.com

Swiss Family Robinson first published as a Children's Classic
in 1993 by Wordsworth Editions Limited
8B East Street, Ware, Hertfordshire SG12 9HJ

This edition first published in 2018

ISBN 978 1 84022 764 2

Text © Wordsworth Editions Limited 1993

Wordsworth® is a registered trademark
of Wordsworth Editions Limited,
the company founded in 1987 by
MICHAEL TRAYLER

Typeset in Great Britain by Antony Gray
Printed and bound by Clays Ltd, St Ives plc

CONTENTS

CHAPTER I

The Shipwreck

[Among those who suffered from the effects of the French Revolution of 1789 was a pastor or clergyman living in the west of Switzerland. He had lost all his property, and therefore resolved to become a missionary. For this purpose he first came to England with his wife and four sons, and soon afterwards accepted an appointment in the mission to Otaheite (the largest of the Society Islands, situated in the North Pacific, and now belonging to France). With a number of other passengers he set sail, intending, after a time, to proceed to Port Jackson, in New South Wales, and settle there. He and his friends took care to provide themselves with such tools, seeds, plants, farm implements, and cattle as they could not purchase in the colony. All went well for a considerable time; but when near the Equator the vessel was assailed by a tempest of almost unexampled severity, and driven out of its course, and it is at the moment when its fierceness was at its height that the story begins.]

The tempest had lasted six long and terrible days. On the seventh, far from diminishing, it seemed to redouble its fury. We were driven far to the southeast, out of our course, and no one knew where we were.

Everyone was worn out and exhausted with fatigue and long watching; and all hope of saving the ship had disappeared. The masts were broken and the sails rent; the ship, full of water, threatened every moment to go down, and each one, commending his soul to God for mercy, strove to find some means of saving his life.

My boys clung to their mother, and trembled with fear in our little cabin. 'My dear children,' said I, 'God can save us if it is His will: if not, we must calmly yield our lives into His hand.'

My poor wife wiped her tears, and, to give courage to her boys, became calm. But while endeavouring to comfort my family, I could scarcely restrain my own grief.

We all knelt together, and offered prayers to the Almighty. Fritz, my eldest boy, prayed most earnestly that God would save his dear parents and brothers, seeming quite forgetful of his own safety. All at once, above the roar of the wind and waves, I heard the cry, 'Land, land!' whilst at the same instant so violent a shock was felt, that I believed the ship had struck on a rock, and would immediately go to pieces. The cracking timbers, and the sudden rush of water which poured in on all sides, proved that I was not mistaken. Then the voice of the captain was heard in terrible tones, above the tumult, shouting, 'Lower the boats! We are lost!'

'Lost!' I exclaimed, and the cry went like a dagger to my heart; but the piteous cries of my children told me that I must not allow them to despair at this awful moment. 'Keep up your courage!' I cried, cheerfully: 'we are all above water yet: I will go on deck at once, and see whether some way of deliverance may not be left for us.'

I went quickly above; but I was immediately thrown down, and wave after wave washed over me, dashing me to the deck. I struggled to withstand their force by clinging to the side of the ship, and then what a sight presented itself!

One boat was far out to sea, and the last of the sailors, as he leaped on board the other boat, cut the rope and it began to drift away. I cried, I begged, I entreated them to return and take my wife and children, but in vain. My voice was drowned in the howling of the blast; and, even had I been heard, the fury of the waves rendered the return of the boats an impossibility. Glancing around me in despair, I observed, with returning hope, the position of the vessel. The bow had sunk forward, leaving the stern, in which was our cabin, high above the water, and as the wreck was fixed between two rocks, there seemed to be no immediate danger of its sinking, especially if the storm abated. Looking towards the shore, which a misty rain obscured from view, perhaps making it appear more barren and desolate than it was, I determined to make an effort to reach that place of safety; and returning to my dear ones below in the cabin, I addressed them hopefully.

'Take courage, my children,' I exclaimed on entering, 'all is not yet lost. The ship is fixed between the rocks, and our little cabin is high above the water. If tomorrow brings a calmer sea, we may be able to get on shore.'

My boys received this news with transports of joy; but my wife noticed my anxiety in spite of my calmness; though I knew that her confidence in God was unshaken, and this gave me new courage.

Searching in the steward's room for provisions, my wife soon had a plentiful supper prepared for us, 'For,' said she, 'nourishment for the body gives strength to the spirit, and we may have a very disturbed night.'

And so it proved. The three younger boys retired to rest, after enjoying a hearty meal, and were soon fast asleep, overcome with fatigue and excitement, but Fritz, the eldest, a youth of fourteen, preferred to watch with us.

During the night the storm continued, and the waves broke over the lower part of the ship with undiminished fury. From time to time a cracking noise told us that the timbers of the wreck were strained by their force, and a continual trembling caused a dread that the vessel might at any moment fall in pieces.

After one of these shocks Fritz exclaimed, 'Father, I have thought of a means of safety. Do you think we could find swimming belts on board for mother and the boys, or make something to support them in the water? You and I could swim on shore; but they cannot swim.'

'An excellent idea, my boy,' I replied. 'We will search at once.'

But no swimming belts could be found; so I determined on a plan which I hoped would prove successful. In the steward's cabin we found a number of empty barrels strong enough to keep a person afloat. These we fastened together in pairs, with space enough between them to allow of their being tied under the armpits of the three boys and my wife. We also provided ourselves with knives, string, a tinder box and matches, and other useful and portable articles, which we could secure about our persons, hoping that, if the vessel went to pieces, we might be able to reach the shore, partly by swimming, and partly by being borne on the waves, and not quite destitute.

Fritz, being now worn out, fell fast asleep. My brave wife and I remained awake, trembling at each shock that threatened to engulf us. It was a trying night for us both; and we passed it in prayer and consultation about our future. With thankful hearts, we hailed with delight the first glimmer of dawn, and, as the wind was considerably abated, we felt somewhat reassured and more hopeful of safely reaching land.

CHAPTER II

Preparations for Escape

I quickly roused the boys. We all assembled on deck, and then, for the first time, they saw that we were alone on the ship.

'O, papa! where are the sailors and the other passengers? How are we to get to land? Are they gone? Why did they not take us?' exclaimed they.

'My children,' I said, 'though we seem deserted, we must not despair. Let us bestir ourselves and each cheerfully do his best.'

'The sea is quite calm enough for us to reach the land by swimming,' said Fritz.

'Swimming is right for you,' answered my second son, Ernest, 'but not for us who can't swim.'

'Suppose we search the ship, and see if anything can be found for a raft,' I replied, after several plans had been proposed.

All dispersed at once in different directions. I descended first to the provision-room, where, to my great satisfaction, I found a good supply of both food and water. My wife and her youngest boy went to visit the animals; Fritz ran to the armoury; whilst Ernest sought for the ship-carpenter's tools. As Jack opened the door of the captain's cabin two large dogs sprang out, and bounded upon him so roughly that they threw him down, and made such boisterous demonstrations that he thought they were about to devour him. He recovered himself quickly, and seizing the largest dog by the ears, jumped on his back and rode gravely to meet me, as I came up the hatchway.

One by one the various explorers returned with their prizes, each bringing what he considered most useful in our position.

Fritz brought with him two guns, some powder, shot, and bullets. Ernest held in his hand his hat full of nails and a hammer and hatchet, while from his pocket protruded a pair of pincers;

whilst little Frank, the youngest, carried a packet of fishing-hooks and lines, with which he seemed much pleased.

'As to myself,' said my dear wife, 'I am the bearer of good news. There are still alive on the ship a cow, an ass, two goats, six sheep, a ram, and a sow.'

'Well done,' I said; 'but I am afraid you have brought two tremendous eaters, Jack, instead of useful things.'

'Not at all, papa!' exclaimed Jack. 'When we get to land the dogs will help us to hunt.'

'No doubt,' I replied; 'but how are we to get there?'

'Easy enough,' said Jack. 'Can we not sail in tubs, as I used to do on the pond at home?'

'A capital idea!' I exclaimed. 'Come, and let us begin at once, and see what can be found in the hold.'

We soon found four large empty casks, exactly suited to my purpose, and I at once set to work to saw them apart through the middle. After great exertion we succeeded, and I contemplated with much satisfaction the eight half-casks ranged in a row on the deck.

'I never dare venture on the open sea in one of these,' said my wife, with a sigh.

'Do not alarm yourself so soon, my dear wife,' I replied. 'My contrivance is not yet finished, and you will find that these tubs are much to be preferred to a shattered wreck which is a fixture on the rocks.'

After another search I got a long, flexible plank, and upon this nailed my eight tubs. Two other planks were nailed firmly on each side of the tubs, and brought together at the ends, forming a stem and stern. I thus made a narrow boat, divided into eight compartments, all strong and well fitted; but, to my dismay, it was so heavy that we were not able to move it an inch.

'Run and bring me one of the capstan bars,' I cried; 'I must use it as a lever.'

Fritz went to find one, while I set to work to saw up a spar into short rollers, which Fritz placed underneath as I lifted the lower part of my boat with the iron bar.

I next fastened a rope to this tub-raft with a strong knot,

attaching the other end to a beam; and then, giving the end a slight push, we had the pleasure of seeing our little craft slide from the deck into the sea. She descended with such velocity that had I not taken the precaution to securely fasten the rope, she would have been carried far out of our reach. Unfortunately, the boat leaned so much on one side that it would have been dangerous to embark in her. I saw at once what was wanted, and quickly gathering up all the heavy things around me, I threw them as ballast into the tubs, and the boat gradually righted itself. But something more was required to make her perfectly safe, and I determined to fix two outriggers similar to those employed by various savage tribes. I securely fastened two topsail yards – one over the stem, the other across the stern – in such a manner that they would not be in the way when we pushed off our boat from the wreck, and fixed the end of each yard into the bunghole of an empty brandy cask. By this contrivance the boat was balanced and kept steady during our short voyage, and nothing now remained but to find some oars for use on the morrow.

I took the precaution to make my boys fix the empty cans and flasks to their arms as a means of safety should anything happen to the ship, and persuaded my wife to dress herself in sailor's clothes, as being more convenient for swimming should she be thrown into the water.

Though she objected greatly at first, I finally convinced her of the safety the dress would prove in case of accident, and she retired to make the change. When she reappeared I could not help paying her a compliment, for the dress became her admirably. With bright hopes for the morning we all retired to our berths, and peaceful sleep prepared us for the exertions of the coming day.

CHAPTER III

Once More on Land

At break of day we were all astir; for hope, like care, is not a friend to sleep. After kneeling together in prayer, I said to my children, 'I hope now, with God's help, we shall soon be out of danger. But first let us provide food and water enough for the poor animals, to last them several days; we may perhaps be able to return for them. And then, my boys, gather together everything you can find that may be of use to us.'

My plan was to take with us a keg of powder, three fowling-pieces, muskets, pistols, and a stock of bullets, with a bullet-mould and lead to prepare more when these were gone. To my wife and each of the children I gave a game-bag filled with provisions.

I loaded two of the tubs with an iron pot for cooking, a fishing-line and rod, a chest of carpenter's tools, and enough canvas to make a tent.

When all was ready for us to embark, I placed each of the boys in a tub, and prepared with my wife to follow them into the boat. All at once the cocks began to crow, as though to reproach us for deserting them.

'I think we might manage to take them with us,' I said, 'for if we cannot feed them, they will feed us.' A couple of cocks and ten hens were accordingly placed in the tubs, and covered over with pieces of wood, to keep them from jumping out. As there was not room for all the poultry, I set free the ducks, geese, and pigeons, hoping that they would reach the land, either through the air or by water.

At length, all being ready, I cut the cable. In the first tub was my wife and little Frank; the three next contained the ammunition, the sailcloth, the tools, the provisions, and the chickens;

Fritz, Ernest, and Jack occupied the fifth, sixth, and seventh; and I took the last one for myself, hoping that I might be able to guide the vessel by the stern oar, which served for a rudder, to a safe landing place.

The tide was flowing as we quitted the wreck, and helped to carry us towards the land. As we glided into the open sea the two dogs, Turk and Juno, which had been left on the wreck, whined piteously, and sprang into the water and swam after us. Both were of large size, so we dared not take them on board, and I feared they would not be able to swim for such a distance; but by now and then resting their forepaws on the poles which formed the outriggers, they managed to follow us without much trouble.

Our passage, though tedious, was safe, for the sea was calm, and we found ourselves gradually approaching the shore. The water was strewed with chests, casks, and bales of goods – the debris of the ill-fated ship – and Fritz and I managed to lay hold of two hogsheads with our oars, and fastened them with ropes to the raft.

As we drew near the coast the land, which presented at a distance a very uninviting aspect, lost much of its wild and sterile appearance; and Fritz declared that he could distinguish various trees, and was certain some of them were palms and coconuts.

I was now beginning to regret that I had forgotten to bring the telescope from the captain's cabin, when Jack drew from his pocket a small one, and offered it to me with delight. By its aid I presently observed a narrow bay, in the direction of which our ducks and geese were rapidly swimming in advance of us, as if to lead the way. We plied our oars bravely, and a strong current assisted in carrying us towards the rocky shore; but I succeeded in guiding our boat towards the entrance of the creek, and found the water just deep enough to float it. After some little trouble, we arrived at last at a low shady bank, on which it was easy for us to land.

Everyone leapt out joyfully from the boat. The dogs, which had already reached the land, bounded with joy, leaping and barking around us in the wildest manner. The geese and ducks quacked to welcome us, and the cries of flamingoes, who flew away as we appeared, mingling with the screams of penguins perched on the rocks, formed a strange concert.

Kneeling down on the shore, our first act was to thank God for our merciful escape, and to commend ourselves to his protection for the time to come.

All briskly commenced unloading the boat, and I set about choosing a suitable spot on which to erect a tent as a shelter for the night. This we did by taking one of the poles which had served to balance the boat, and firmly fixing it upright in a hole in the ground. One end of another pole was then tied crossways, near the top of the first one, whilst its opposite end was fixed in a hole of the rock.

Over this framework we stretched our sailcloth, fastening it to the ground with a number of pegs; whilst for greater security our chests and other heavy articles were placed around the edge of the cloth to keep out the wind. Fritz attached hooks to the edges in front, that we might draw them together during the night. This being done, I sent the children to gather moss and grass to spread in the tent for our beds.

CHAPTER IV

The First Day on Shore

While they were thus busy, I piled up a number of large stones at a little distance from the tent, and on the margin of a little stream, to form a fireplace. Gathering several armfuls of dried twigs and branches of trees, I placed them on my stone hearth, and soon had a cheerful blaze. Upon this I placed our iron pot full of water, and into it my wife dropped several of the tablets of portable soup she had brought with her from the ship.

Meanwhile Fritz, who had loaded his gun, proceeded along the banks of the stream to look for game. Ernest sauntered towards the sea; while Jack scrambled among the rocks to search for shellfish.

Having now a little leisure to look about me, I returned to our landing place to secure the two hogsheads we had taken in tow. I discovered, however, that the spot on which we landed was inconvenient for unloading, as it was too steep. While I stood considering what was best to be done, I was alarmed by hearing Jack cry out as if in terror. Seizing a hatchet, I ran to his aid, and found him wading up to the knees in a shallow pool, where an enormous lobster* had seized him by the leg in

---

* There are several species of lobster found in various parts of the world, but the best edible ones inhabit the waters of the temperate regions of the northern hemisphere. They live in the clearest water, hiding in the crevices of a rocky bottom. Lobsters, like crabs, change their shell every year. Previous to this process they appear sick, languid, and restless, and lie motionless. Three or four days are required before they acquire their new shells. While in the soft state they increase in size, the new shell being about a third larger than the old one. When one of their limbs is broken off, either by accident or fright, a new one grows in its place in the course of a few weeks, but it is never so large as the original one. The general colour of the lobster is black: in boiling it changes to red.

one of its claws, resisting all his attempts to get rid of his enemy.

I jumped into the water, and, striking a blow at the creature with my hatchet, soon brought it maimed to shore, to Jack's great delight.

He laid hold of it with both his hands and set off to carry the captive to his mother. Scarcely had he grasped it, however, when it struck him such a violent blow with its tail that he threw it on the ground and began to cry.

I could not help laughing outright at the little fellow's misadventures, and in his anger he took up a stone and stunned the creature by a blow on the head.

Finding the lobster helpless, Jack ran with it to his mother, exclaiming, 'Mother, mother! Ernest! Frank! see, I've caught a lobster – such a large one! Where is Fritz?'

Everyone congratulated him on his success, and listened with astonishment at the recital of the perils he had encountered in securing the prize. Ernest suggested that the creature should be at once cooked for dinner, but his mother decided that it should be set aside till we had more need of it.

'I think,' said Ernest, 'I have discovered something quite as good to eat as Jack's lobster; but I did not care to get any, because I should have had to wade through the water.'

'What an excuse!' exclaimed Jack. 'Afraid of getting wet! – and they were only nasty mussels, I dare say, and not fit to eat.'

'I believe they are oysters,'* replied Ernest, quietly; 'and they are not at any great depth in the water.'

'And pray, why did you not bring us some? Every sort of wholesome food is now acceptable. And to fear getting wet! how

* There are numerous species of oyster found in the shallow seas or river mouths of all temperate and warm climates, but those found on the British coasts are the best. Oysters breed in April or May, and the fry, or fertilised eggs, are called spat. This spat adheres to pieces of wood, stone, old oyster shells, &c., and the young oysters become fit to eat in about a year and a half. 'Natives', as they are called, are grown in artificial beds, and our largest supply is provided in this way.

absurd! You see that the sun has dried my clothes and Jack's already,' said I.

'I did not think about that, papa,' replied Ernest, 'or I could have brought salt as well. I saw a great quantity in the fissures of the rocks, produced by the evaporation of the sea-water, I suppose.'

'Doubtless, my little philosopher. Go and bring some, unless you would like to eat your soup without it.'

In a short time he returned with what was evidently common salt, but so mixed with sand that it seemed to be of no use.

'I can improve it,' said my wife, 'by dissolving it in fresh water, and straining it through a piece of linen. If the water is allowed to evaporate or dry up, the salt will remain behind.'

'Why could we not use sea water?' asked Jack.

'Because it would be too bitter,' replied Ernest.

The soup was now ready, but Fritz had not returned. Where could he be? While we waited, my dear wife remarked, 'How are we to eat our dinner, now that it is prepared? We have neither spoons, plates, nor cups. We cannot lift this huge pot of boiling soup to our mouths.'

We all laughed heartily, especially when Ernest said, 'If we only had some coconuts we could divide the shells in two; they would make splendid cups.'

'Certainly,' I replied; 'but why not wish for a dozen silver spoons? Wishing is useless: we must invent something.'

'These shells I saw would serve us for spoons capitally,' said Ernest.

'True, my boy. Oyster-shells are better than nothing; run, boys, and get some as quickly as you can.'

Away started Jack. Ernest followed slowly, and when he reached the spot, there was Jack up to his knees in the water. He hastily detached the oysters, and threw them to Ernest, who collected them together (being still very careful not to wet his feet), and they quickly obtained a good supply.

Almost at the same moment as they returned Fritz also reappeared, with one hand behind his back, affecting a dispirited air.

'Empty-handed?' I asked; but his brothers, who crowded round him, shouted, 'A sucking pig! a sucking pig! Did you kill it? Oh, do let us see it!'

Fritz then, with a self-satisfied look, produced his prize, the first result of his hunting exploits. He told us he had wandered to the other side of the stream, and found the vegetation very different – green grass, pleasant meadows, and such magnificent trees to shade us from the heat.

'And, papa,' he added, 'there are chests and boxes and spars floating about, and the beach is strewed with portions of the wreck. Can we not go and get them? If the animals were here that we left on board, it would be easy to find food for them; and how useful they would be, especially the cow, to supply us with milk! Don't let us stay in this barren place.'

'Patience!' I said. 'Not so fast; one thing at a time. Tomorrow we will try what can be done. But tell me, did you see any traces of our shipmates?'

'No, papa; not a sign of them, on sea or land. I think this is an island; there are pigs here, for I have shot one. It is not exactly like the pigs in Europe, for its paws are more like those of a hare. I saw several in the grass, sitting on their hind legs, and feeding themselves like squirrels.'

The agouti

'It is not a pig at all!' said Ernest, who had been examining it. 'It has hair like silk, and four large cutting teeth in front. I believe it is an animal I have read about in my natural history, called an agouti.'*

* The agouti (ă-goo'-tē) is a four-footed animal, about the size and shape of a hare, with a brownish body and a yellowish belly. There are three varieties, all of which are very voracious. The animal burrows in the ground or in hollow trees, and lives on vegetables, doing much damage in the sugar-cane plantations of the West Indies, Brazil, and Guiana, where it is chiefly found. It makes a grunting noise, similar to a pig. Its flesh is white and well tasted.

'I believe you are right,' I replied. 'Its appearance corresponds exactly with the descriptions I have read, as well as with the pictures.'

While we were discussing this question, Jack was endeavouring to open an oyster with his knife. 'Here is a simpler way,' I said, and, placing some upon the hot coals, they quickly opened of themselves.

'See, my children, these are considered a great delicacy. Let us taste them.'

No one, however, cared to eat the oysters: so we threw away all but the shells, which we used instead of spoons, plates, and basins.

While we were making a good meal, the dogs discovered Fritz's agouti, and began tearing it to pieces before we observed them. Perceiving this, Fritz seized his gun (the first thing he could lay hold of) and struck at them with it so violently as to bend it. The poor beasts ran off howling, and he then threw stones after them so long as he thought he could reach them.

My voice recalled him to himself, and, when his rage calmed down, I talked seriously to him about giving way to such ungovernable passion. He looked much ashamed, and owned he was wrong, and presently, after begging his mother's pardon, I observed him trying to make friends with the dogs by offering them some biscuit.

The sun was low in the horizon before we finished our meal. The fowls and ducks gathered round us, and my wife gave them some corn from a bag I had seen her throw into the tub alongside of little Francis. I commended her forethought, but at the same time urged her to feed the birds on biscuit-crumbs, and to keep the corn for sowing. The pigeons retired to certain holes in the rocks and the fowls roosted on the top of the tent, while the ducks and geese sought shelter in the marshy margin of the river. We, too, made preparations for the night. Loading our firearms, we placed them so as to be at hand in case of alarm, and, having offered up our evening prayer, withdrew to our tent and lay down to sleep. To the great surprise of the children, it was almost immediately dark, from which I guessed we were somewhere near the equator, or at least within the tropics.*

I looked out once more to make sure that all was right, and then closed the entrance to our tent. The day had been warm, but it was now intensely cold,† and we were glad to creep close together for warmth. The children were soon asleep. My wife and I kept awake for some time; but sleep crept over us insensibly, and our first night on shore was passed quietly and without alarm.

* When the sun sinks perpendicularly below the horizon, as he does in the tropics, there is little or no twilight. Twilight is caused by the reflection of sunlight from the higher parts of the atmosphere, which are still illuminated after the sun has sunk so far below the horizon as to be invisible from ordinary heights. Twilight is considered by astronomers to last until stars of the sixth magnitude become visible to the naked eye. The morning twilight is called dawn.

† In the tropical regions, after the sun has set, the heat accumulated by the earth during the day rapidly radiates into space, and intense cold, if the air be clear and the sky free from clouds, is frequently felt.

CHAPTER V

A Tour of Discovery

The crowing of the cocks aroused us at early dawn, and my wife
and I consulted together on our future proceedings We agreed
that it was our first duty to search for some trace of our late
companions, and also to explore the country, before deciding
upon our future resting-place. My wife understood readily that it
would be impossible for the whole family to venture on such a
tour, and she proposed that I should take Fritz, as he was the
strongest and most useful, and leave the younger boys under her
care at the tent. I therefore begged her to prepare breakfast
while I aroused the boys.

They were soon awake, and I enquired of Jack what had
become of his lobster.

While he ran to bring it from a crevice in the rock, where he
had placed it for safety beyond the reach of the dogs, I told
Fritz of our proposed expedition, and I added, as Jack returned,
'I think you ought to give up to Fritz the claws of the lobster
which I promised you, to provide him with a dinner on his
journey today.'

'An excursion, an excursion!' they all cried. 'Are we going,
papa?' and they began to jump and dance round me like young
kids, clapping their hands with joy.

'Not this time,' I said. 'We know not what dangers we may
meet. Fritz and I have strength to bear the fatigue of a long
journey. You must stay here with your mother, in safety. We
shall take Turk with us, and leave the other dog Juno to defend
you.'

I desired Fritz to take his gun, an axe, and a game-bag; and
equipped myself in the same manner. I likewise placed two small
pistols in his belt, and also loaded the game-bag with powder

and shot, some biscuits, and a bottle of water.

Breakfast was ready by this time. It consisted of the lobster and some biscuits. What remained over we pocketed for our journey, and, kneeling together in prayer, we asked for the succour and protection we all so much wanted now.

At last we parted from the family in tears, and I heard them calling after us words of encouragement and apprehension till we reached the stream which we intended to cross.

The banks of the river rose abruptly, and we were obliged to follow the stream for some time before we found a spot at which to cross.

After walking a long distance we noticed a narrow part, and contrived, by leaping from stone to stone, to reach the opposite bank in safety.

The aspect of the country changed entirely, and we had forced our way scarcely a hundred yards through the tall rank grass when we heard a rustling behind us. I stopped, and, looking round, saw the unknown enemy, which proved to be our trusty dog Turk. We had forgotten to call him, and he had been sent after us, doubtless by my thoughtful wife.

Pursuing our journey, we reached the seashore. Here we paused, and gazed anxiously in every direction across the ocean, in the hope of discovering the boats containing our unfortunate companions, but in vain: not even in the sand could we find any trace of the footsteps of man.

'Why should we trouble ourselves about them at all?' asked Fritz. 'They cruelly abandoned us.'

'My dear boy,' I replied, 'we ought always to return good for evil. If they could not be useful to *us*, we might help them greatly, for they carried nothing away from the wreck, and may be perishing of hunger.'

Thus talking, we continued our walk, and at the end of two hours reached the entrance of a wood. Here we halted to rest, seating ourselves under the cool shade of some trees by a rippling brook.

Suddenly Fritz started up, saying he was sure he saw a monkey among the foliage; and the loud barking of Turk confirmed him in his idea. He ran forward to assure himself that he was right, and while looking up, regardless of his steps, he struck his foot violently against a round, hard substance which lay on the ground.

Picking it up, and bringing it to me, he said, 'What is this, papa? I think it must be the nest of some bird.' I smiled as I replied, 'It is a nut, my boy – a coconut, too.'

'Some birds make round nests, I know,' he persisted.

'Certainly they do, but this is not a nest. The coconut has two shells: the outer one forming a thick fibrous covering, and the inner one hard, and containing a milky fluid. Break it, Fritz, and you will find the real nut or kernel inside.'

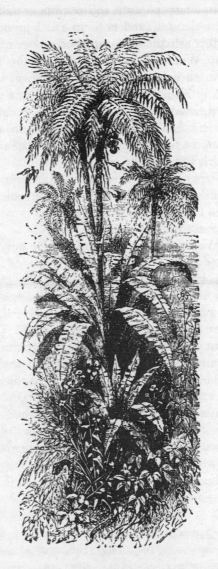

The coconut palm

He obeyed; but the nut was evidently an old one, and, instead of finding a pleasant and refreshing milk inside, the kernel was quite decayed, and unfit to eat. I proposed that we should go farther into the wood, and perhaps we might meet with a fresher one. We had not proceeded far before we found another, sufficiently fresh to afford us a pleasant repast.

A little farther on the wood became so thick and overgrown with lianas* that we were obliged to cut our way through with the hatchet. We again emerged on the seashore, and saw scattered here and there single trees of a remarkable appearance, which attracted the notice of Fritz.

'Papa, look at those trees with large bulbs growing on the trunks,' he cried. 'How absurd they look!'

As I drew nearer, I found, to my great satisfaction, a group of calabash trees, loaded with fruit.

'What can those singular-looking bumps on the stems be?' he asked.

'Gather one of them,' I replied, 'and let us examine it.'

Immediately he placed in my hands a common gourd. 'This gourd, Fritz,' I said, 'has generally a hard dry shell, of which cups, plates, and bottles can be made. The flexible stem of the plant on which it grows winds itself about the trunks and boughs of large and strong trees, from which the gourd is suspended, for without this support the weight of the gourd would break the branches of the plant on which it grows.'

After a little talk about the use of the gourd, I explained to him how the savages form the shell into bottles, spoons, and other articles; and we then set about making some dishes and plates. I showed him a better way of dividing the gourd than with a knife. Tying a piece of string tightly round the shell, I struck at it with the handle of my knife till a slight incision was made; then,

---

* Lianas (*lī-ä'-năs*), sometimes called lianes (*lī-änz'*), are the climbing and twisting plants of tropical forests, which wind themselves round the trees, often stretching from one to the other, making the passage through the forest extremely difficult. The honeysuckle and clematis of our hedgerows are familiar examples, on a small scale, of similar plants.

tightening the string, the nut was soon separated into two equally-sized bowls. He had spoiled his own by cutting it irregularly with his knife.

Filling our newly-made dishes with sand to prevent them from shrinking, and leaving them to dry in the sun, we set forward again, and after walking for nearly four hours, we arrived at a neck of land which stretched far out into the sea, ending abruptly in a small but steep hill. Up this we climbed with some difficulty; but, when we reached the summit, the calm ocean lay stretched before us, sparkling in the sunlight; on our left appeared a small bay; while the rich verdure of the land extended almost to the water's edge.

After gazing with delight on this fertile spot, we examined with our glass the vast expanse of sea; but no trace of our companions could be discovered, and no habitations of man nor signs of his presence could be observed inland.

The thought that we were alone saddened me; but I remembered we had left our dear home and country with the intention of settling as colonists in a distant and strange land, and that while we could go nowhere without meeting difficulties – though we certainly did not expect to be so entirely alone – the home allotted us might have proved destitute of many advantages which seemed within our reach.

We now descended the hill, and perceived at a little distance a grove of palm trees;* but to reach it we had to cross let large space thickly grown with tall reeds. Advancing cautiously, for at

---

* Palms are generally tall, slender trees, often of gigantic height, without branches, bearing at the summit a magnificent crown of very large leaves. The stem is always woody and hard towards the outside, and the root fibrous. The centre is soft, often containing, when young, a large quantity of starch (as in the sago palm); and when old, strong fibres, which can be easily separated. Palms are mostly natives of tropical countries, tropical America producing a greater number than any other part of the world. The coconut palm is most widely distributed. About 600 different kinds are known, and scarcely one of them but has some good and useful property. Thus, wine is made from the juice of the Palmyra Palm, called palm-wine or toddy; palm-oil is the produce of another

every step we feared that we should tread upon snakes or other venomous reptiles, I made Turk go before; and, as a further means of defence, cut from the reeds, which were tall and thick, one of the strongest I could find, to carry in my hand.

Soon, to my astonishment, a glutinous juice ran between my fingers. I touched it with my lips, and its sweet taste proved at once that we had discovered a grove of wild sugar-canes.

Wishing Fritz, who was a little in front of me, to make the same discovery, I advised him to cut a reed as a protection.

He obeyed at once, and commenced striking the reeds right and left with it to frighten away serpents. In so doing he split the cane, and the juice streamed over his hand. Without a word he tasted it, and, jumping for joy, cried, 'Oh, papa! papa!

Palm trees

---

tree; wax of another (growing in great abundance on the Andes), sago from the soft centre of another, and sugar from the fruit of another. The *askes* of another furnish salt; whilst the hard kernel of another provides vegetable ivory. Thread, weapons, utensils, food, and building materials are all furnished in abundance by the leaves and stems. The coconut and date palm are valued for their fruits; the cabbage palm for its young leaves: and the fan palm, and many others, for its foliage, whose hardness and durability render it an excellent material for thatching.

a sugar-cane!* Only taste it! Oh, how delicious! how delightful!'
he continued, eagerly sucking at the cane.

'I should like,' he said, 'to
take some of these to my
mother and brothers, as well as
a few to refresh ourselves on
the way.' I advised him not to
take too many, so he cut a
dozen of the largest, and, stripping them of their leaves, carried them under his arm. We
soon arrived at the thicket of
palm trees, when a number of
monkeys, startled by our footsteps and by Turk's barking,
rushed up the trees, where they
sat grinning and chattering.
Fritz, without a moment's reflection, threw down his bundle of canes, and raised his gun;
but I restrained his hand, and

The sugar-cane

* The sugar-cane is a tall, handsome grass, 18ft to 20ft high, with hard-jointed
stems, large, firm, and thin leaves, and numerous flowers gathered in a tuft at
the top of the stem. It is probably a native of India, the West Indies, or China,
but is now extensively grown in both the East and West Indies. The canes are
cultivated from cuttings, and take about a year to come to perfection. They are
then cut down close to the ground, and are crushed between heavy rollers in a
mill, so as to extract all the juice. This juice is boiled, and afterwards placed in
shallow vessels to cool. It is then put into hogsheads with holes in the bottom,
through which the molasses, or treacle, drains, leaving what is called raw sugar
behind. The West Indies, Brazil, Guiana, and Java at present furnish our chief
supplies of sugar. Much of the sugar now sold in England is made from
beetroot, the manufacture being carried on in France, Germany, Holland,
Austria, Belgium, and Russia. In Canada and the United States sugar is made
from the sap of the sugar maple.

showed him the folly and cruelty of killing a poor animal that could be of no value as food; and which also excited no just apprehension of danger.

'Just see how useful they can be to us,' I said. Accordingly I picked up some stones and threw them, but not high enough to reach the monkeys. Their rage at this increased to fury, and presently they seized the coconuts within their reach and flung them down upon us in a perfect hail, so that we had to save ourselves, as we best could, in the shelter of the trees, or by jumping aside to avoid the by no means well aimed missiles. Fritz laughed heartily at the success of my stratagem, and, when the coconut shower had ceased, we gathered as many as we could conveniently carry.

We now sought for a suitable spot in which to enjoy the repast thus provided. We broke the outer shells with one of our hatchets, and by making a hole with a knife at stalk end of the kernel, and another on the opposite end, we were able to drink the milk. After breaking the inner shell, we found a white part inside, which, being easily scraped off with our new spoons, proved very agreeable eating. The juice from the sugar-canes completed our delicious feast.

The remains of the lobster were given to Turk, with a few biscuits, and as he did not appear satisfied, we threw him some pieces of the sugar-cane and coconuts, which he pounced upon eagerly and seemed to enjoy immensely.

I now gathered together such of the coconuts as had long stalks, and tied them together to enable me to carry them more easily. Fritz took up his bundle of sugar-canes, and we began our homeward march.

CHAPTER VI

The Return Home

Fritz soon found the weight of his canes more than he expected: he shifted them from one shoulder to another, then carried them under his arm, and finally halted, and sighing deeply, said, 'Really, papa, I had no idea that a few reeds would be so heavy.'

'Never mind, my boy,' I answered, 'patience and courage! Let us each take a fresh staff; and then fasten the bundle crosswise on your gun.'

We did so, and as we went along I often tasted my cane; Fritz tried to do the same, but found he could not extract any juice. 'How is this, father?' he said.

'Think a little,' I replied, 'and I am sure you will find the reason; you do not yet employ the right means.'

He soon discovered that he must make a small hole above the first knot of the cane to let in the air. This done, he was able to refresh himself as much as he wished with the delicious beverage.

'But,' said he, 'if we continue to use them as we are doing, very few of the canes will reach the tent.'

'Do not let that trouble you,' I replied, 'for the heat of the sun will most likely turn the juice sour.'

'At any rate,' replied Fritz, 'mother will enjoy the cocomilk, for I have filled my tin flask.'

'My dear boy, you may find a bottle full of vinegar instead of milk by the time we reach home; it quickly spoils.'

'Shall we try it now?' he asked.

The bottle was taken from his bag; and, as we endeavoured to draw the cork, it flew out with a loud report, the milk following it foaming like champagne.

We tasted it, and found it very delicious. Much refreshed, we walked on so briskly that we soon reached the place where we had left our gourd dishes. We found them quite dry, and very light and easy to carry. Scarcely had we reached the edge of the wood when Turk darted past us, barking furiously at a troop of monkeys,* who were gambolling on the turf. They were taken completely by surprise, and sprang into the trees out of Turk's reach. All escaped but a female monkey, who carried a little one on her back, and could not get away. Turk had seized the poor animal, and although Fritz rushed to the rescue, he arrived too late to save her. The baby monkey had fallen on the grass when

Turk seized its mother, but the instant the little one caught sight of Fritz, it jumped nimbly upon his back, and held on firmly by the boy's hair.

Seeing there was no danger, I could not help laughing heartily at the ludicrous scene.

By coaxing and gentleness, I succeeded in relieving poor Fritz of his unwelcome guest,

The ape

* The name monkey is not, strictly speaking, a scientific term, but includes roughly all those creatures which, in their general appearance and structure, somewhat resemble man. They are properly divided into three classes: apes, four-handed animals (the hind limbs of all monkeys terminate in hands, not feet) having no tail, and no cheek pouches; baboons (chiefly found in Africa), having elongated muzzles like a dog, cheek pouches, and deep-set eyes, and generally short tails; and monkeys, which possess long prehensile tails and short muzzles, with cheek pouches. The species of the monkey tribe are very numerous. Many are found in the Malay Archipelago and India, but the largest number inhabit the forests of Africa and South America. The chimpanzee, gorilla, and orang-outang are apes. The drill and mandril are baboons. This species rarely exceeds the size of a mastiff. Apes and baboons are generally fierce and untractable, but some of the former are tractable and gentle. Monkeys generally live together in herds in the forests, and eat fruit, leaves, insects and eggs. The worship of apes and monkeys has been common among pagan nations from a period of remote antiquity, and still prevails very extensively, being practised in some parts of Japan and India and by some of the African tribes.

which was no bigger than a kitten, and incapable of taking care of itself. I took it in my arms as I would an infant.

'It is very obvious the little orphan has chosen you for its adopted father, Fritz,' I said jokingly.

'The little rogue!' laughed Fritz. 'What a jolly little fellow it is. He has pulled my hair terribly. But do let me keep it. We can feed it with coconut-milk, or, if we get the cow and the goat from the ship, there will be milk to spare. And perhaps, if he lives, his instinct may help us to discover if the fruits and vegetables we find are wholesome or poisonous.'

I could not help regarding it with pity, for it must inevitably perish if abandoned by us. I therefore consented, on condition that he took entire charge of it and taught it to be obedient, and we continued our walk. Turk soon overtook us, and at the sight of him the little monkey crept into Fritz's bosom, much to his inconvenience. But a lucky thought struck him: he tied the monkey with a cord to Turk's back, and though the dog was very rebellious at first, we at last induced him to submit quietly to his burden. Beguiling the journey with an entertaining conversation on the habits of monkeys, we proceeded slowly homeward. I could not help anticipating the mirth of my little ones when they saw us approach like a couple of showmen with animals to exhibit.

Juno was the first to salute us by her barking. Turk responded, and so alarmed his little rider that he sprang from the dog's back to the shoulder of Fritz, and nothing could induce him to quit his seat there. Turk, finding himself free, set off to rejoin his comrade, and, crossing the river by swimming, announced our approach.

My dear ones soon assembled on the opposite bank to welcome us, and, full of joy and affection, our happy party was once more united.

The children, who were impatient to examine what we had brought back, began shouting, 'A monkey! a monkey! Oh, Fritz! where did you find it? What a funny little fellow! I wonder what it can eat. But what are those sticks for? And look at those curious things papa is carrying!'

When the first transports of joy were over, I said, 'I am truly thankful to see you all again. We have returned in safety, thank God, and have brought you many good things; but we have not succeeded in finding any trace of our lost companions.'

'Let us be grateful that we are united once more,' said my wife: 'we can still be happy in our own society and love. Now let us relieve you of your burdens.'

Jack accordingly took my gun, Ernest the coconuts, Frank the spoons and plates which I had made, and my wife the game-bag. Fritz distributed the sugar-canes among them, and again placed the little monkey on Turk's back, to the children's great amusement.

Ernest appeared so laden with the nuts that his mother, out of pity, took them from him.

'If Ernest only knew what he had given up,' said Fritz, 'he would soon ask for them again – they are coconuts.'

'Coconuts!' he exclaimed. 'Oh, mamma, give me them again. I can carry them and the gun, too.'

'No,' said his mother, 'one thing is enough, or I shall hear you complaining presently how the load fatigues you.'

'But I can throw away these sticks and carry the gun in one hand.'

'Throw away those sticks!' cried Fritz, 'I advise you not. They are sugar-canes!'

'Sugar-canes! sugar-canes!' exclaimed they all, as they clustered around Fritz, who showed then how to suck the juice.

Thus conversing we reached the tent, where I found an appetising supper awaiting us. On one side of a large fire stood the iron pot full of soup. From a piece of wood, which rested on two forked sticks fixed in the ground, hung a goose roasting, while large oyster-shells underneath formed the dripping-pans. Several kinds of fish were cooking on the hot stones; and, best of all, at a little distance was one of the hogsheads I had saved from the wreck, which my wife and the boys had contrived to drag up from the riverside and open. It contained a number of Dutch cheeses wrapped in thin sheets of lead.

'You have not been idle during our absence, I see, my dear children; but was it not a pity to kill one of our geese?'

'I believe it is a penguin,* papa,' said Ernest; 'and I call it a booby, because it let me kill it so easily with a stick.'

'Come, now,' said his mother, 'do you not see how Ernest's eyes are fixed on the coconuts? Let him taste one of them.'

'Certainly,' I replied; 'and the monkey must not be forgotten.'

'But he will not eat anything, papa,' said Jack. 'I have tried him with all I can think of.'

The Penguin

'We must try him with the milk of the coconut,' I said. 'Probably he will drink that.'

We all seated ourselves on the grass, with the spoons and dishes made from the calabash tree. I broke open two of the coconuts, and all enjoyed the white lining of the inner shell, after I had extracted the milk. Nor was the monkey forgotten, for the boys dipped the corners of their handkerchiefs in the milk, and were delighted to find that the little creature would suck them eagerly.

---

* The penguin (*pen-gwin*) is an aquatic bird (of which there are several species), found solely in the southern hemisphere, chiefly in high latitudes; but one species extends into the warm regions of Peru. It is web-footed; is covered with close, short feathers and its hind legs are set far back. Its short wings, destitute of quills, but covered with a scaly skin, are useless for flight, but are valuable aids for swimming and diving. The bird is found in prodigious numbers on the Antarctic coasts, as many as 30,000 or 40,000 having been seen together. They do not seem to fear the presence of man, and are easily captured. They make no nest. The female lays one egg on the shore, which is carefully tended by both the male and female bird until it is hatched. The flesh of the young birds is considered good eating. Their voice is loud and harsh – between a grunt and a bray. Fish forms their chief food. The auk is the representative of this bird in the northern hemisphere.

While we were enjoying the fish, which was very good, Fritz begged his mother to taste the coconut champagne.

'Taste it first yourself, Fritz,' I said. He did so, and was mortified to find it had turned to vinegar.

'As I expected, my boy; but, never mind, vinegar is very good with fish;' and as I poured some over my plate the rest followed my example.

By the time we had finished, the sun was rapidly sinking, and it was necessary to prepare for the night. My wife and the boys had collected a large quantity of dry moss and grass, which was now spread on the floor of our tent, and formed comfortable beds.

The poultry were already gone to roost as before, and the geese and ducks had betaken themselves to their night-quarters. After offering our evening prayer, and arranging all things as on the previous night, I entered the tent. Fritz and Jack took the little motherless ape between them, to protect him from the cold, and we were all soon fast asleep.

We had not slept long before the restless movements of the fowls and the barking of the dogs awoke us all. Seizing my gun, I rushed out, followed by my wife and Fritz, who were also armed.

We perceived, by the light of the moon, that a battle was going on between a couple of jaguars* and our brave dogs. Already the dogs had nearly settled one of their assailants; but the other one, hoping to take them at a disadvantage,

The jaguar

* The *jaguar* (*ja-gwar'*), or American tiger, is the largest and most formidable of the American beasts of prey. It is found in all parts of S. America, from Brazil to the Isthmus of Darien. It is about the size of a wolf, and is therefore smaller than the tiger. It is marked with dusky spots or rings, with a dark spot in the centre of each. Its food consists of all sorts or animals, from insects and shellfish to oxen and horses, but it rarely attacks man unless pressed by hunger. It is sometimes called the ounce.

still pressed on them, though the two courageous animals kept him at bay.

Fritz and I fired together and laid one dead; the other one, frightened by the report of the guns, made off. By my leave, Fritz dragged the dead one into the tent, to show in the morning to his brothers, whom neither the firing of the guns nor the barking of the dogs had wakened. We lay down once more and slept soundly until the crowing of the cock in the morning, when my wife and I awoke to consult about the business of another day.

CHAPTER VII

A Voyage to the Wreck

'What shall we undertake first today, my dear wife?' I said. 'A voyage to the ship is absolutely necessary, if the cattle are to be saved from starving; and there are many useful things on board that would be of real value to us. But we have also very much to do here; and above all things it is necessary that we construct a more secure dwelling.'

'Certainly a voyage to the wreck is first necessary, for, should a storm arise, everything on board will be lost; but patience, dear husband,' she replied, 'all will be accomplished in time.'

It was accordingly agreed that the three youngest boys should stay with my wife, and that Fritz and I should proceed to the wreck.

I soon roused the children. Fritz jumped up first, and ran for his jaguar. He placed it on its four legs in a most lifelike attitude at the entrance of the tent, to surprise his brothers. No sooner did the dogs see it than they rushed at it to tear it in pieces, but Fritz called them off. Their barking, however, caused the boys to hasten out to see what was the matter. Jack issued first with the monkey on his shoulder; but no sooner did the little creature see the jaguar than he sprang into the tent and hid himself among the moss, till only the tip of his little nose was visible. All were astonished to see this large animal. Francis thought it was a yellow cat, Jack said it was a tiger, and Ernest pronounced it a panther.*

---

* The panther is a ferocious animal, about the size of a large dog. It is covered with short hair, of a yellow colour, and is marked with darkish spots. It lives on small animals, and will even climb trees in pursuit of them. Naturalists now suppose the panther to be only a variety of the leopard. It is found in all the warmer parts of Asia and Africa. The animal corresponding to it in America is called the puma.

Fritz laughed at the learned professor, who knew the agouti immediately, and now called a jaguar a panther.

The panther

At last I interfered. 'You are none of you very far wrong, for the jaguar partakes of the nature of the cat, the tiger, and the panther.'

My words produced peace, and after assembling once more for prayer we proceeded to breakfast. We were obliged to content ourselves with dry biscuits, which were so hard that our teeth could scarcely break them. Fritz asked for some cheese, and went behind the tent to procure some from the cask.

Ernest followed, and quickly returning with a bright face, exclaimed, 'Oh, papa, if we could only open that other cask!'

'What cask?' I asked.

'The large cask just outside. Some grease has run through a little crack. I am sure it looks exactly like salt butter.'

'Come, boys,' I exclaimed, 'we will go and see;' and all sallied out to examine this wonderful cask. I very quickly proved that the boy was right, and in a few minutes obtained a coconut-cup full of beautiful salt butter. We toasted the biscuits at the fire, covered them with butter, and so had a most delicious breakfast. During our meal the dogs lay quietly by our side, and did not seem at all anxious for their share of our breakfast. I examined the poor beasts, and found that they had been bitten in several places, especially about the neck.

As the animals commenced licking their wounds, my wife washed the salt out of some butter and applied it as a salve, and in a few days they were completely healed. Ernest remarked that they ought to have spiked collars, to defend them from any wild beasts they might encounter.

'I will soon make them two collars,' said Jack, if you will let me.'

I was glad to employ his inventive powers; and requesting my children not to leave their mother during our absence, we set about the necessary preparations for our voyage.

While Fritz made ready the boat of casks, I erected a flagstaff, attaching a piece of sailcloth to it for a flag, to serve as a signal to us that all was going on well. If, however, we were wanted, they were to lower the flag, and fire a gun three times, when we would immediately return; for, as I informed my dear wife, it might be necessary for us to remain on board all night. Trusting to find provisions on the ship, we took nothing but our guns and ammunition. Fritz asked to be allowed to take the little monkey, that he might give it some milk from the cow or the goat.

After taking a tender leave of each other, we embarked, and rowed into the middle of the bay. Here I perceived a strong current from the river, which set in toward the vessel. I was glad to take advantage of it, and it carried us a long way on our voyage. We rowed the remainder of the distance, and soon moored our boat alongside the wreck, and went on board.

Fritz hastened first to feed the cattle, and all the animals saluted us with manifest joy. We put the young monkey to a goat, which, to our infinite amusement, he sucked with extraordinary grimaces. We then took some refreshment ourselves; and Fritz proposed that we should at once fix a mast and sail to our boat. 'For,' said he, 'the current which helped us to the vessel cannot carry us back; but the wind, which was against us, will be of immense service if we have a sail.'

I thought his advice good, and we immediately began this work. I selected a strong pole for a mast, and made a hole in a plank to receive it. Securing the plank on our fourth tub, thus forming a deck, we raised our mast, and finally fastened it by ropes to each extremity of the boat. Fritz ornamented the top of the mast with a little red streamer, and gave our boat the name of *Deliverance*. To complete its equipment, I contrived grooves for inserting an oar, so that I could steer and otherwise manoeuvre the boat from either end.

As the day was already far advanced, I signalled to my wife that we should not return that night; and we spent the rest of the day in emptying the tubs of the stones we had used as ballast. In their places we stowed such useful things as powder and shot, nails and tools of all kinds, pieces of cloth, and, above all, knives, forks, spoons, and kitchen utensils, including a roasting-jack. In the captain's cabin we found a service of silver plate, some pewter covers and dishes, and a small hamper filled with choice wine. All these we took, as well as a stock of provisions, intended for the officers' table, including portable soup, Westphalian hams, and Bologna* sausages, together with some bags of maize, wheat, and other seeds, and a supply of potatoes.

We also collected all the implements of husbandry we could find room for, and stowed them in the boat; together with some hammocks and blankets. Of all these things there was an ample supply, so we had free choice among an immense quantity of useful articles, all suitable for the isolated life we seemed likely to have to spend on this lonely island. As our vessel was an emigrant ship, whose destination was the southern seas, our fellow-passengers had provided themselves with provisions and utensils which a ship bound on an ordinary voyage would not have carried.

To all these I added a barrel of sulphur, with which to make matches; all the cord and string I could lay hands on, and a large roll of sailcloth. Our tubs were loaded to the edge, and, if the sea had not been so calm, it would have been dangerous to attempt our return.

We once more exchanged signals with those on shore, to assure ourselves of their safety, and after prayers, retired to our tub-boat for the night. Fritz slept soundly; but I, anxiously thinking of the dangers of the previous night, could not close my eyes. I was, however, thankful for the protection those on shore had in the faithful dogs, in case of emergency.

* Pronounce *bō-lō'-nyâ* (not *bō-lō-nă*, nor *bō-lôg'-nă*).

CHAPTER VIII

The Return Home

As soon as morning dawned, I hasted on deck, and with the help of the telescope, I saw my wife looking towards us, and observed with pleasure the flag, which denoted their safety, floating in the breeze. After enjoying a breakfast of biscuit, ham, and wine, we set about devising some means of saving our cattle. Fritz suggested a raft, but even if we could contrive one sufficiently large, how were we to get all the animals to remain still on it?

At last Fritz proposed swimming belts, and we spent two hours in making and fixing them. For the cow and ass it was necessary to have an empty cask on each side, well bound in strong sailcloth, fastened by leather thongs over the back and under each animal. For the rest, we merely tied a piece of cork under their bodies; and fastened a cord to the horns or neck of each animal, with a slip of wood at the end for a convenient handle. And now came the difficulty of launching our living freight into the sea.

Luckily, the waves had already broken a large hole in the side of the ship, and left an opening wide enough for the cattle to pass through. We therefore led them to the lower part of the ship, and made the first experiment by giving the donkey a push into the water. He fell with great force, and rose struggling to the surface, but quickly recovering himself, he floated away in grand style.

The cow was of far more value than the ass. I felt very anxious about her; but I pushed her in gently, and with equal success.

We managed easily to get the whole afloat, excepting the sow, who resisted furiously. When at last she was forced into the water, she swam quickly away, and made for the shore, which she reached long before the rest.

We now embarked, and discovered the advantage of our mast and sail, for the wind carried us gently toward the shore; loaded as we were, we could never have rowed our boat.

Suddenly a loud cry from Fritz filled me with terror.

'Father!' he exclaimed, 'we are lost! See what an enormous fish! It is coming towards us!'

The bold boy had seized his gun, and by my directions aimed and fired at the head of a monstrous shark as it was preparing to seize one of the sheep. It immediately plunged and disappeared, leaving a long red track of blood behind, which showed that it was severely wounded.

I again took the rudder, and, as the wind blew favourably towards the bay, guided the boat to a convenient landing-place. We set the animals free from the guiding-ropes, and they all scrambled safely on shore.

There was no sign of my wife or children; but a few moments afterward they appeared, and, with a shout of joy, ran towards us. We were thankful to be once more united, and proceeded to release our herd from their swimming-belts, which, though so useful in the water, were exceedingly inconvenient on shore, after which we sat down to recount our adventures.

Fritz, Ernest, and I next began the work of unloading our craft; while Jack, seeing that the poor donkey was still encumbered with his swimming-belt, tried to free him from it. But the donkey would not stand quiet, and the boy's fingers were not strong enough to loosen the cordage; he therefore scrambled upon the animal's back, and trotted towards us.

'Come, my boy,' I said, 'no one must be idle here, even for a moment; you will have riding practice enough hereafter. Dismount, and come and help us.'

Jack was soon on his feet. 'But I have not been idle all day,' he said. 'Look here!' and he pointed to a broad belt of yellow skin round his waist, in which he had stuck a couple of pistols and a knife. 'And see,' he added, 'what I have made for the dogs!' The dogs came at his call, and I saw that each of them was provided with a collar of similar material, stuck full of nails, which bristled round their necks in a most formidable manner.

'Well done, my boy!' said I. 'Where did you get your materials? and who helped you?'

'He had no assistance,' said my wife; 'and as for the materials, Fritz's jaguar supplied the skin, and the needles and thread came out of my wonderful bag.'

Fritz expressed his annoyance at hearing that Jack had cut up the jaguar's skin; but I reminded him that he must act like a man, and not show anger at little things. Besides, on nearing the tent, he discovered that the body of the animal was already becoming offensive, and he was glad to help to drag it down to the sea, and so get rid of it.

By this time the unloading of our boat was nearly accomplished, and we started for our tent.

Finding no preparation for supper, I said, 'Fritz, go and bring the Westphalian ham from which we breakfasted out of the tub.'

Fritz soon got the ham, and carried it to his mother triumphantly, while Ernest set before me a dozen white balls with parchment-like coverings, which they had found during their morning's ramble.

'Turtles' eggs!'* said I. 'Well done, Ernest!'

While my wife prepared supper, we returned to the boat and brought up the remainder of our cargo, collected our herd of animals, and again repaired to the tent.

An excellent meal awaited us. My wife had improvised a table of a board laid on two casks, and on this was spread a white

---

* The turtle is a reptile more or less flattened from above, enclosed in a case formed of two leathern or scaly shields, and having horny jaws in the place of teeth. Instead of feet it has four long and broad paddles adapted for swimming. These creatures are found in the seas of all warm countries, and they feed mostly on marine plants. They swim with great ease and come to land to lay their eggs, which they do in the sand several times in the year, to the number of from 150 to 200 each time. There are several species. The most important is the green turtle, which is found in the tropical parts of the Indian and Atlantic Oceans, being especially abundant near Ascension I. It is from six to seven feet long, and its flesh is a most valuable article of food. The plates forming the carapace (as the horny covering is called) of the Hawk's Bill Turtle furnish tortoise shell. The name tortoise is properly given to those species that live entirely on the land.

damask tablecloth, on which were placed knives, forks, spoons, and plates for each person. A tureen of good soup first appeared, followed by a capital omelette, then slices of the ham, and finally some cheese, butter, and biscuits. After we had regaled ourselves,

The turtle

I requested my wife to relate her adventures during my absence.

'The first day,' said my good Elizabeth, 'I spent in anxiety about you, and attending to the signals but this morning, being satisfied that we had nothing to fear, I began to look about for a shady and sheltered spot for our tent. I believe this barren shore has not a single tree, so I decided to search for a more comfortable spot for our residence, and determined to set out with the children on a journey of discovery across the river. We took our game-bags and hunting-knives, and the boys each carried a gun and a stock of provisions, whilst I had a large flask of water and a small hatchet. The dogs went before, Turk evidently considering himself our guide; and, with some difficulty, we crossed the river. I now saw the advantage of your having so early taught the boys to use firearms, as our defence depended almost entirely on two boys of ten and twelve years of age.

'We reached the hill you described to us, and I was charmed with the smiling prospect; but I was determined to make our way towards a beautiful and shady wood we had in view. It was a

most painful and harassing progress through grass and reeds that
were higher than the children's heads. All at once we were
startled by a strange rustling sound, and a bird of large size rose
and flew away, before the boys could get their guns ready. They
were much mortified, and I recommended them to have their
guns in readiness, for the birds would not be likely to wait till
they loaded them. "I am sure," said Francis, "the bird must be an
eagle, it was so large;" but Ernest ridiculed the idea, and thought
it more like a bustard.* They were getting into hot discussion on
the subject, when suddenly another bird of the same kind sprang
up close to our feet, and was soon soaring above our heads. I
could not help laughing to see the look of confusion with which
the boys followed it with their eyes. At last Jack took off his hat,
and making a low bow, said, "Pray, Mr Bird, be kind enough to
pay us another visit; but adieu for the present." We searched for
and found the large nest they had left. It was very rudely formed
of dry grass, and was empty. Some fragments of eggshells were
scattered near, as if the young had been recently hatched. We
therefore concluded that they had escaped among the grass.

'Chatting together, we at last reached the grove. Numbers of
unknown birds fluttered among the high trees, and seemed to
welcome us with their song. We found, however, that what we
thought a wood was merely a group of a dozen trees, but of a
height far beyond any I had ever seen, with trunks apparently
springing from roots which formed a series of supporting arches.
Jack climbed one of the arches, and measured the trunk of a tree
with a piece of string; he found it to be thirty-four feet round. I
made thirty-two paces round the roots. Between the roots and
the lowest branches it seemed about forty or fifty feet high. The

* The bustard is the largest of European birds, often weighing 30lb, with a
breadth of wings of 6 or 7 feet. It was formerly common in England and
Scotland. It is found in the open plains of the South and East of Europe, the
steppes of Tartary, in India, South Africa, and Australia. It feeds on green corn
and other vegetables, and frogs, worms, and insects. There are several species,
all of which run fast, but as they fly with difficulty, they escape, when disturbed,
by alternately running and flying.

foliage was abundant, the branches thick and strong, and the leaves of a moderate size, resembling our walnut tree. A thick, short, velvety, turf carpetted the ground beneath and around the roots of the trees inviting us to repose, and altogether this was one of the most delightful spots the mind could conceive.

The great bustard

'Here we sat down and made our noonday meal. A clear stream which ran near furnished its agreeable waters for our refreshment. I was so delighted with the spot that I could not but think that if we could contrive a dwelling on the branches of one of these trees, we should be in perfect peace and safety. On our return we took the road by the seashore. We found a large quantity of timber, chests, and casks floated from the wreck, all too heavy to bring home; but we succeeded in dragging and rolling several of these waifs from the vessel up the beach. Our dogs; in the meantime, employed themselves in fishing for a kind of crab, which they appeared to eat with relish, and I now saw they would be able to furnish their own food. As we rested from our hard labour, I saw Juno scratching in the sand, and swallowing something with great avidity. "They are turtles' eggs," said Ernest. We therefore drove away the dog, and gathered about two dozen of them. While we were depositing this unexpected prize in our provision-bags, we were astonished at the sight of a sail. Ernest said he was certain it was papa and Fritz, though Frank feared it should be the savages who visited Robinson Crusoe's island, coming to eat us up. We were soon, however, enabled to calm his fears. Hastening to the river, we crossed it by leaping from stone to stone, and arrived at the landing-place, to greet you on your safe return.'

While listening to my wife's narration of the day's adventures, night came on. We knelt together in prayer, and then arranged ourselves in our places as usual, sleeping soundly and with great comfort upon the mattresses and under the soft coverlets which I had brought from the wreck.

CHAPTER IX

Building a Bridge

Next morning my wife and I rose early, and took counsel together as to our future proceedings.

'I have been considering your plan,' I said, 'and I think we ought not hastily to change our abode. We are protected, in case of danger, on all sides by the sea, the rocks, and the banks of the stream; and, most important of all, we are near to the ship, which is still a mine of wealth to us.'

'All very well,' answered my wife, 'but you do not know how unbearable is the heat. It is so suffocating in the tent as to make me anxious about the children's health; and our only refreshment is the mussels and oysters which we gather on the shore As for the safety you prize so much, did it save us from the jaguars? The treasures on board the vessel are not to be despised, I know; but I would renounce them gladly to be spared the anxiety your sea voyages to secure them occasion me.'

I acknowledged there was some force in the arguments of my wife; but 'I think we can make a compromise,' I said. 'I will consent to change our residence to your favourite trees on condition that we retain this settlement among the rocks as a provision-store and as a kind of fortress to which we can retire in time of danger. If this plan be adopted, the first thing we must do is to throw a bridge across the stream, so as to make communication between the two places quite easy.'

'A bridge!' exclaimed my wife in astonishment. 'The construction of a bridge will be a tedious labour. Could we not load the ass and the cow with our baggage and cross the river as we did before?'

I assured my dear wife that she was exaggerating both the difficulty of the work and the obstacles that stood in our way, and she acknowledged at last that I was right. We therefore decided that the work should be commenced at once, 'For,' said she, 'I am anxious to leave this place as soon as possible.'

The boys were quickly aroused, and, on hearing the plan of bridge-building, were full of eager anticipation and delight. After breakfast, Fritz took the monkey to the goat for his morning feast. Jack slipped away to the cow, and tried to milk her into a gourd; but, as he could not succeed, his mother took the vessel and showed him how to do it. As Jack saw how cleverly she drew the milk, he said, 'Ah, if I had only known how to do it like that! But I mean to learn, and then I can help mamma.'

In the meantime I prepared our boat for a voyage to the ship, to obtain planks and beams for building the bridge, and as soon as breakfast was over, I set off with Fritz and Ernest; for, as it was necessary to accomplish our purpose quickly, double help was needed. Rowing out to sea, we soon got into the current of the stream we had already found so useful. Passing an islet at the entrance of the bay we saw a number of gulls,* albatrosses,† and other sea-birds, congregated about some object on the shore. Fritz prepared to fire among them; but I forbade him. I knew so extraordinary a gathering must be caused by something unusual, and I was anxious to find out what it was. I hoisted the sail to take advantage of a slight breeze that had sprung up, and we soon reached the islet.

We then discovered that it was the carcase of a monster fish which had been cast ashore, on which the birds were regaling themselves so eagerly that they did not notice our approach until we were within gunshot of them.

* The gull is a web-footed and long-winged sea bird. There are several species, which are found on the shores of all latitudes. They assemble in flocks, are great gluttons, and very courageous. They frequent the ledges of the cliffs, where they build their rough nest and lay their eggs.

† The albatross is the largest of the web-footed sea birds, often measuring more than 17ft from tip to tip of the extended wings. It is capable of long flight, and is often seen at great distance from the land. It frequents the Southern Ocean, and is also found in large numbers in the Bering Strait.

'Why, Fritz,' cried Ernest, 'this must be the shark* you shot yesterday!'

'Indeed it is, Ernest,' said Fritz, not a little proud of his achievement.

The gull   *The albatross*

Ernest drew out the ramrod of his gun, and struck at the birds right and left. Some were so voracious that they refused to abandon their prey, and were knocked down and killed. We cut off a few strips of shark's skin, which I thought might prove useful to us, and then returned to the boat.

But this was not the only fruit of our visit to the island, for I saw with joy that a number of planks and beams had been loosened from the wreck, and cast on the sands by the waves. They were admirably adapted for my purpose, and would thus save me the trouble of seeking them on the vessel. So I determined to select those most suitable for building our bridge,

* The shark, a species of fish of large size, and very voracious, is found in all but the coldest seas. Its body is long, and the mouth, which is large and wide, and armed with several rows of very sharp teeth, is situated beneath the head. The white shark, the most formidable of the species, is often found 30ft long. The rough skin is dried, and often employed by joiners to polish wood. A kind of leather called shagreen is made from the untanned skin. (Horse, ass, and camel skins are also used for the same purpose.)

and, with the help of the two boys, we soon had them afloat and fastened with ropes to our boat. Once more we put to sea, and presently lay alongside our old landing place, having returned in less than four hours from the time we started. We were not expected, and none of our dear ones were there to welcome us. I shouted, however, to attract their attention, and they soon came running, Frank with a fishing-rod over his shoulder and Jack with a number of large lobsters in a handkerchief.

Little Frank, with pride, began at once to explain that he had first discovered them, while Jack related how he had courageously waded into the water to get them. I congratulated both the boys on the success of their exertions, and felt thankful that food for our wants was thus provided day by day.

Turning in the direction of the stream, I proceeded with the boys to decide upon the most suitable place for the erection of the bridge. Jack suggested a spot, and I was anxious to see if he had made a wise choice. 'If you have,' said I, 'we will immediately set about bringing up the planks, while your mother prepares our repast.'

After a careful examination, I was of opinion that the place was well suited for the purpose, and offered very few difficulties. We therefore set to work at once to transport the materials thither.

The ass and cow were of the greatest help to us in this task. Calling to mind the simple harness in use by the Laplanders with their reindeer, I yoked the ass by simply passing the loop of a rope round its neck, and then, carrying it through between its legs, I secured it to a piece of timber which I wished to draw ashore. The cow was, in a similar manner, harnessed by a rope attached to its horns, and we were thus able, with moderate difficulty, to drag the materials for the bridge to the chosen site.

By means of a piece of string, with a stone tied to one end, which we threw to the opposite bank, we were able to measure the width of the stream, and soon discovered that the distance from one side of the river to the other was eighteen feet. As it was necessary that the beams should have at least three additional feet resting on each shore to make the structure secure, this would require the under ones to measure about twenty-four feet. Fortunately we found several which, as they exceeded this length fully answered our expectations.

But how to get such long and heavy pieces of timber across the water was the next difficulty to be grappled with: for we were thoroughly fatigued with the labour we had already undergone. While considering the subject, my wife announced dinner, and we returned to the tent for rest and refreshment.

Our good housekeeper had boiled for us a dish of lobsters, which was very tempting, and prepared some rice. But before beginning she asked us to inspect two immense bags, which she had made out of a piece of sailcloth, and had sewed with packthread. As she had no needle large enough to hold the thread, she contrived to stitch the edges of the canvas together, using a nail for an awl, and by patience and perseverance had finished two first-rate saddlebags to hang across the donkey's back like panniers, each of which would contain a great quantity of articles when we changed our home.

I praised my dear wife for her ingenuity, and we all despatched our dinner in haste and hurried back to our work.

As we approached the spot, a feasible plan suggested itself which I immediately put into execution. I secured one end of a beam to the trunk of a tree, at about four or five feet above the ground, and to the other attached a long rope, to which a stone was tied for throwing it across the river. I next crossed to the opposite bank and adjusted a pulley to another tree, through which I drew the rope, and then returned with the end in my hand.

To this end I harnessed the cow and the ass; then, passing the beam round to the front of the tree, I led the animals away from the water. As they moved slowly forward, the beam gradually rose, swung across the water to the opposite side, and then, when I checked my novel pair of draught horses, it sank steadily into its place on the bank.

Fritz and Jack at once sprang boldly on to the beam, and danced lightly and rapidly across this narrow bridge, somewhat to my alarm.

The most difficult part of the work was now over. The second, third, and fourth beams soon followed, and were arranged at equal distances from each other. Across these we laid planks of about eight or nine feet long, but did not nail them firmly, as I wished to be able to remove them quickly in case of danger, to prevent the passage of enemies, whether men or wild beasts.

The bridge seemed in every point perfect: the supports were firm, and the passage across complete; and I now summoned my wife to examine what she had persuaded herself was to be the labour of a lifetime. Both she and the children were astonished to see so difficult a piece of work accomplished so easily. The boys jumped about, clapping their hands and shouting triumphantly at the top of their voices, and we all ran over it backwards and forwards several times, in our joy and excitement.

The great exertion had exhausted our strength; and, as evening approached, we knelt once more to offer our thanks to God for His merciful care of us during the day, and retired to rest.

CHAPTER X

The Land of Promise

Next morning, after breakfast was finished, I immediately commenced preparations for our journey, warning the children of the necessity for caution and prudence (as we knew not what enemies we might encounter), and urging them to keep together in case of danger or of attack.

Our first act was to load the ass and the cow with the travelling-bags containing our provisions, tools, cooking-utensils, hammocks, blankets, and other useful things.

All was ready; but my wife would not consent to leave the poultry as food for the jaguars: above all, little Francis must have a ride: he could not possibly walk all the way. I soon made him a comfortable place between the bags on the back of the ass, whilst the children ran to catch the poultry and pigeons, but with no success whatever. Their mother, by scattering some handfuls of grain within the open tent, soon decoyed them into the enclosure, where, when the curtain was closed from the outside, they were easily caught. Their wings and feet were tied, and they were all safely placed in two hampers, one on either side of the donkey.

All the things that we left were laid up in the tent which was well barricaded with casks and boxes, both full and empty. Each of us carried a bag for provisions, a gun, and some ammunition. Fritz marched at the head of our procession with his mother, followed by the cow and the ass and his rider. The goats, led by Jack, with the little monkey on the back of his foster-mother, formed the third detachment. Ernest followed with the sheep, and I walked last as the rearguard. The dogs rushed here and there as our adjutants, making it their business apparently to see that all was right.

As the procession moved on slowly, I explained how our

Eastern fathers were wont to travel thus from place to place, and that even now the people of Tartary and Arabia, and other nomadic races, follow this sort of life. 'But, for my part,' said I, 'I shall be glad when our wanderings are over.'

Thus conversing, we arrived at the bridge, and at this point the sow joined our procession. We had found it impossible to make her follow the other animals; but when she discovered that we had really left her, she hastened to overtake us. We crossed the bridge without accident, the sow grunting her disapproval of the whole affair.

But now difficulties beset us. The grass looked so fresh and tempting that our troop scattered themselves right and left to feast upon it, and we should have been unable to place them again in rank and file but for the help of our faithful dogs, who, barking and chasing, brought them again into order. To avoid a second interruption, I directed our leader to turn to the left, and take the way along the coast, where the tall rank grass was not so tempting to the animals.

We had scarcely started when the dogs suddenly darted into the thick grass; and presently their furious barking became mixed with howls of pain, as if they were struggling with some fierce assailant.

Fritz hastily advanced to the spot, presenting his gun, followed by Jack, while Ernest, who was nervous and timid, ran behind his mother, yet making ready to fire in case of danger. I followed the boys anxiously, with my gun in readiness.

They reached the spot before me, and the next moment Jack cried out, 'Papa, come, quick! a huge tapir!'*

I saw, as I hastily approached, that he was right, and that the dogs were busy assailing it.

---

* The tapir is an animal about the size of a small ass, found in all parts of South America. Its skin is brown, and its flesh, though dry, is considered good eating. It has hoofs like the hog, and a muzzle lengthened into a short proboscis or trunk. It partakes of the nature of a pig and a rhinoceros. It is a harmless creature, and lives in the forest. A larger species is found in the forests of Sumatra and Malacca.

Jack, without thought of consequences, drew his pistol from his belt, and shot it dead; then, giving way to a burst of boyish exultation, he called upon us to help to convey his prize to his mother. Taking his pocket-handkerchief, and fastening one corner round its neck, he ran off, dragging it after him, to where his mother awaited us.

The tapir

'Look, mamma!' he cried. 'Isn't this a beautiful prize? I killed it myself with my pocket-pistol. I was not at all afraid.'

His mother praised him for his courage and skill, and we then resumed our march.

Without further accident, we at last arrived at what we had already styled 'The Land of Promise'. The beauty of the spot exceeded the description which had been given to me, and I congratulated my wife on her discovery of this charming place.

'Oh, what magnificent trees!' exclaimed Ernest. 'Look at their height!'

'Indeed, they are magnificent!' I cried. 'This is a truly wonderful place. If we can establish our selves upon these trees we may feel secure, and shall have little cause to dread the attack of any wild beast.'

We released the animals from their load, and set them free to graze with the sheep and goats, first tying their forelegs together loosely, that they might not wander far. The sow we left to do as she pleased; whilst the fowls and pigeons, to their great relief, were also set at liberty, and left to choose their own retreat.

We seated ourselves on the soft green turf to consult upon the arrangements for our future dwelling-place, when suddenly we heard the report of a gun just behind us; a second shot followed, and in a few moments Fritz appeared, carrying by its hind-legs an enormous tiger-cat.

'Bravo!' I cried. 'You have rendered good service to our fowls and pigeons. Your friend there would have made sad havoc in our farmyard in a single night. But tell me, Fritz, how you managed to kill this beast of prey, and where did you find him.'

'I saw a movement among the foliage of a tree. I went quietly and stood at the foot, and there on a branch I saw this monster. The first shot brought him to my feet, but he was not dead, and, as he tried to rise, I fired a second time, and he moved no more.'

'You may think yourself fortunate,' I said, 'that the creature did not fly at you after the first shot. I think the one you have just killed is a species very common at the Cape of Good Hope and in South America. It is frequently called the margay,* and is so voracious, that even our sheep and goats would not be safe against such a formidable enemy.'

'Can we not make use of its beautiful skin?'

'Indeed you can,' I replied. 'From the legs you can make cases for knives, forks, and spoons, and of the tail a hunting-belt in which to carry your pistols.'

This so took the fancy of the young people that they gave me no rest till I had shown them how to remove the skin both from the wild cat and the tapir.

Meanwhile Ernest and little Frank were busily employed, one in gathering stones to make a cooking-place, and the other in collecting dry branches of trees for a fire.

Presently little Frank appeared with his arms full of dry wood, and something in his mouth, which he was eating with a great relish.

'I've found something so nice!' he cried – 'oh, so nice!'

'My child, what are you eating?' cried his mother. 'It may be poisonous.'

Frank, in a fright, allowed his mother to take from his mouth what appeared to be the remains of a small fig.

'Where did you get this?' she asked.

'Yonder, in the grass,' replied Frank. 'There are thousands of

* The margay or tiger-cat is a small species of leopard, found in South America. It is very destructive to small quadrupeds and birds, but may be easily tamed. Several species of tiger-cats, called by various names, inhabit tropical countries.

The tiger cat or margay

them. The fowls and the pigeons are eating such a lot! and the one I tasted was so nice, that I thought it wouldn't do me any harm.'

'Do not be alarmed,' I said to my wife, as she looked at me enquiringly. 'These trees are apparently a species of mangrove,* and bear a kind of fig, which I believe is wholesome: as a rule, moreover, we may consider safe any kind of vegetable or fruit

---

* The mangrove is a tree found in both the East and West Indies. The bark is used for tanning in Brazil, and from the fruit a light wine is made. There are many species, most of which send down roots from their branches. They grow in the mud about the mouths of rivers and on the margin of the sea, even to low-water mark.

eaten by birds or monkeys. But, Frank,' I continued, 'you must never eat the fruit you find, or even taste it, till you have shown it to me.'

Frank heard my statement about the monkeys and ran off to present a fig to Master Nip, who seized it hastily, and began eating it with the most comical expressions of delight.

I divided the tapir into halves: one to be eaten fresh, the other salted, and the flesh of the tiger-cat we gave to the dogs. Until dinner was ready I employed myself in planning our castle in the air. I thought of making a ladder of ropes; but this would be useless, if we did not succeed in getting a cord over the lower branches to draw it up. As neither my sons nor myself could throw a stone (to which I had fastened a cord) over these branches, which were thirty feet above us, it was necessary to think of some other expedient. In the mean time, dinner was ready, and we truly enjoyed the flesh of the tapir and the excellent soup my wife had made for us from it, with biscuit as a substitute for bread.

CHAPTER XI

The Dwelling in the Trees

When we had finished our dinner, I prepared our night-quarters by first hanging the hammocks from the arched roots of the tree, covering the whole with sailcloth, so as to make a temporary tent, which would at least keep off the night damps and noxious insects.

My wife then busied herself in preparing some harness for the animals, as I intended to employ them the following day in drawing the beams up to our tree. This done, I walked down to the beach with the boys to search for pieces of wood suitable for building our new abode. For some time we hunted in vain, finding nothing but rough driftwood, utterly unfit for our purpose. Ernest at length pointed out a quantity of bamboos* half-buried in the sand, which were exactly what I wanted. Stripping them of their leaves, I cut them into lengths of about five feet each; these I bound in bundles to carry to the tree, and having secured some slighter one to serve as arrows, we set about searching for some flexible boughs.

I presently saw what I required in a thicket at a little distance. As we approached the marsh, Juno suddenly started forward among the underwood, barking furiously. Immediately a flock of fine flamingoes,* which she had put to flight, rose into the air

* The bamboo is a kind of grass, of which there are many species, all round in tropical countries, many of which attain a great size. Some stems grow from 5in to 6in in diameter and 50ft or more high, and are so hard and durable as to be used for building, for all sorts of furniture, for water-pipes and many other purposes. Thatch is made of the leaves of some species. In China the soft inner part is made into paper and the leaves are plaited into hats.

* The flamingo is a bird of the stork kind, with long legs and neck, often

A grove of bamboo

with a loud rustling sound. Fritz, always alert and on his guard, instantly fired, bringing down two of them. One fell dead, but the other, which was only slightly wounded in the wing, ran off, and used his long legs, as if he were on stilts, with the greatest

standing from 4ft to 6ft high. When full grown it is of a bright-red colour, hence the name (from L. *flamma*, flame). It lives on small fish and insects. Its long legs prevent it sitting down, so it constructs a heap of mud with a cavity at the top, in which it lays its eggs (which are white and about the size of a goose's), and hatches them by straddling across it. These birds are chiefly found on the muddy banks of rivers, or the marshy shores of tropical coasts, in Asia and Africa. One species is also found in America.

swiftness. I followed, yet should have failed to overtake him had not Juno rushed forward, and, seizing the bird by the wing, held it firmly till I came up.

The flamingo fought bravely for his life, beating me with his wings with great force; and it was only after a struggle that I succeeded in mastering him.

Flamingoes

After securing the bird I picked out such of the canes as had done flowering, and cut off the hard ends to form points for my arrows, which I knew to be the practice among the natives of the Antilles. I also selected a few of the longest I could find to use as measuring rods for calculating the height of our tree.

We now set off back, and presently arrived at our resting-place. Ernest carried the long canes and the bundle of bamboos. Fritz bore the dead flamingo, while I took charge of the living one.

I anointed its broken wing with an ointment made of butter and wine, and bound it up, fastening the bird by a long cord to a stake fixed in the ground near the bank of the stream. In a few days the wound was healed, and the bird, subdued by kind treatment, soon became quite tame and at its ease among us.

'I fear,' said mother, when she first saw the bird, 'that, with so many living animals, we shall find our supply of food quickly disappear.'

'The flamingo,' I replied, 'will not eat grain, like our poultry, but will be quite satisfied with insects, fish, and little crabs, which it will pick up for itself.'

I now set about measuring the height of the tree, and first asked my wife to supply me with a ball of thick, strong thread. Whilst she was searching for what I wanted in her wonderful bag, I sat down on the grass and made a number of arrows from the canes we had gathered, filling them with wet sand, to weight them. One end of each I tipped with the hard points I had cut from the canes which had done flowering, and to the other end I fastened some of the feathers of the dead flamingo. I then made a bow of one of the strongest bamboos, and tying one end of the ball of string to my arrow, fixed it in my bow, and sent it directly over one of the thickest of the lower branches of the tree. Falling to the ground, it drew the thread after it, and by this means I found that at least we should want eighty feet of rope for the two sides of our ladder.

I next fastened a rope to the string, drew it over the branch, and charmed with this result, I at once hastened to complete my ladder. I stretched two ropes on the ground about one foot apart, whilst Fritz cut pieces of cane two feet long, which Ernest passed to me. These I placed about twelve inches apart, ladder-wise, between the ropes, and fastened them at each end – first with a knot, and then with a long nail through both ends, and into the rope, to prevent them from slipping.

In a short time our ladder was completed; and tying it to the end of the rope which went over the branch, we drew it up without difficulty. All the boys were anxious to ascend; but I chose Jack, as the lightest and most active. His brothers and myself held the ladder firm by the end of the cord, and Fritz followed, carrying a bag of nails and a hammer. He secured the ladder so firmly to the branch that I had no hesitation in ascending myself. I carried with me a large pulley fixed to the end of a rope, and attached it to a branch above us, to assist in raising the necessary materials with which to build our castle in the trees. On descending the ladder, well satisfied with my success, and full of confidence for the future, I called Fritz and Jack to come down to help me to collect the animals, and gather wood for a fire to burn all night and protect us from wild beasts.

Supper was now quite ready. One piece of the tapir was roasted by the fire; another piece formed a rich soup; and both smelt delicious. A cloth was spread on the turf, and the ham, cheese, butter, and biscuit were placed upon it. Supper done, my wife assembled the fowls by scattering crumbs and grain to accustom them to the place. The pigeons flew to roost on the higher branches of the trees, while the fowls perched on the ladder; the beasts, we secured to the roots, close to our hammocks. Then, after prayers, I kindled our watch-fires, and we all lay down to rest. The boys were rather discontented, and complained of their cramped position in the hammocks, longing for the freedom of the beds of moss; but I instructed them to lie as the sailors do, diagonally; and soon all sank to rest except myself. I was kept awake by anxiety for our safety, but by degrees I became more composed; at last, overcome by fatigue, I also fell asleep, and only awoke when all the family were astir.

CHAPTER XII

A Castle in the Air

After breakfast, Jack and Ernest put the harness on the cow and ass, and prepared to accompany their mother to the shore, to bring home the driftwood necessary for our house.

Fritz and I then ascended the ladder, and found enough to do. The centre of the trunk from which the curving branches sprang was in every way suitable for our purpose. The lower branches, before they bent downwards, were strong, thick, and close together, and almost horizontal for a considerable length. I decided, therefore, to use them as beams for a flooring.

On the upper branches, a few feet above us, I determined to hang our hammocks, and over those, a little higher up, I decided to stretch a large piece of sailcloth as an awning and roof for our aërial castle. Between the sailcloth and the floor I cleared a sufficient space by cutting away the branches that grew across it, and by the time my wife and the boys returned with their first load we were prepared for them. By means of the pulley and rope we were able to draw up, piece by piece, the wood suitable for our flooring, my wife and the boys acting as the workmen below.

When this platform was completed, Fritz and I erected a handrail around it, with pieces of wood about three feet long, forming an enclosure, so as to make it perfectly safe. Though as yet without walls or ceiling, excepting those formed by the foliage of the tree, our work already appeared like a room. The whole morning was thus occupied, my wife and the boys having, in the meantime, brought up three loads of planks and beams from the beach.

After a slight luncheon we returned to our work, and, slinging up the hammocks on the branches, prepared to raise the sailcloth over all as a ceiling. This was the most difficult part of our task, but by means of the pulley we at last succeeded, and managed to draw the canvas over the upper branches. By fastening its edges on three sides to our handrail, we were able to leave the fourth side (which looked out towards the sea) uncovered, as a means of entrance and light; and before sunset this wonderful resting-place in the tree was completed, and had a most comfortable appearance.

We had still several small planks left which I thought would do admirably for a table and two benches. By nailing several planks on the highest parts of the roots for the table, and on the lower curves for benches, I succeeded in making a most useful piece of furniture.

While my wife prepared supper, of which we all stood in need, the boys lighted the fires for the night. The dogs were tied to the tree as a protection against invaders, and, when all was ready, we commenced our ascent. My three eldest sons soon ran up the ladder; my wife followed with more deliberation and caution, and she also arrived safely at the top. My own ascent was the most difficult, for in addition to having Francis on my back, I had to loosen the lower part of the ladder from the roots, where it was nailed, in order to be able to draw it up after me during the night, so that it swung about very unpleasantly. We retired to our hammocks free from care, and did not wake till the sun shone brightly in upon us at the opening of the tent.

The next day was Sunday. We descended, and breakfasted on warm milk, fed our animals, and then, with my children and their mother seated on the turf, I placed myself on a little eminence, and after repeating the service of the day, which I knew by heart, and singing some portions of the 119th Psalm, I told them a little allegory, in which I sought to develop some of the important truths which serve as the foundation of morality and Christian religion, and we concluded by singing a hymn.

After dinner, I proposed that we should give names to our place of abode and to all the parts of the island known to us, in order that, by a pleasing delusion, we might fancy ourselves in an inhabited country. My proposal was well received, and I further suggested that we should give such simple names as should point out some circumstance or special event connected with the spot, so as to fix it more readily in our memory. Beginning with the bay where we landed, I called on Fritz for a name.

'The Bay of Oysters,' said he: 'we found them in such great abundance there.'

'Oh, no!' said Jack. 'Lobster Bay is a more appropriate title, for there I was caught by the leg.'

'Then we ought to call it the Bay of Tears,' said Ernest, 'to commemorate those you shed on that occasion.'

'Should we not rather name it Safety Bay,' said my wife, 'in gratitude for our escape?'

We were all pleased with this name, and proceeded to give the name of Tent House to our first abode; Shark Island to the little island in the bay; and, at Jack's desire, the spot where we had cut our arrows was named Flamingo Marsh. The promontory from which Fritz and I had vainly sought for traces of our shipmates received the name of Cape Disappointment. The stream was to be Jaguar River, and the bridge, Family Bridge. Our new abode gave us the greatest trouble. I suggested the name of Falcon's Nest, 'for,' said I to my boys, 'you are as hardy and adventurous as young falcons, and as much disposed to deeds of pillage in the immediate neighbourhood of your home'. Many names had been proposed, but mine at once set all the others aside. It was received with acclamation, as being a most appropriate as well as a poetical one.

It was thus that in pleasant gossip we laid the foundation of the geography of our new country, and, closing our Sabbath Day with prayer and a glad hymn of praise retired to rest with peaceful hearts.

CHAPTER XIII

New Discoveries

Early on Monday morning I found that the boys were all longing to have bows and arrows of their own. Our more serious duties had prevented me making for each of them an instrument which I knew would give them all pleasure, and probably be of great service to us.

Ernest had used the bow which I had lent him very skilfully, bringing down some dozens of ortolans* – a kind of woodlark – from the branches of our tree, where they assembled to feed on the figs. These proved a most acceptable addition to our provisions, and indeed a delicacy, that under any circumstances would have been most welcome. Ernest's skill made the boys all anxious to be equipped in like manner.

The ortolan

* The ortolan is a small bird, a native of Northern Africa, which in the summer months resorts to Southern Europe. It is about six inches long, with yellowish plumage on the throat and back, and the upper part of the body brown. It has no song, but makes a continuous chirp, and frequents busy places. Its flesh is considered a great delicacy. Large quantities of these birds, fattened by feeding them on millet, are potted and pickled, and exported from Cyprus. In the West Indies it is called the rice-bird, and in America the rail.

I was glad to comply with their request, as I wished them to become skilful in the use of the arms of our forefathers, which might be of great value to us when our store of ammunition failed. I accordingly made two bows and two quivers to contain a supply of arrows, and, attaching straps to them, armed my young archers.

While Fritz proceeded to finish his skin-case, Jack came to ask my assistance in dressing the skin of the tapir. Having finished the bows and arrows, I first showed him how to clean it with sand and ashes, and assisted him in his first attempts as a currier and tanner.

Having got rid of any fat or loose pieces of flesh that adhered to the skin, I directed him to rub it with butter, and stretch the skin with his hands to give it flexibility, and as Jack decided to make a cap for himself out of it he stretched it over the roots of the tree to dry.

Thus employed the morning passed and dinner-time drew on. As the heat was somewhat less oppressive towards the latter part of the day, I proposed we should walk to Tent House to renew our stock of provisions, and endeavour to bring the geese and ducks to our new residence, where there was a stream well-suited to their habits. Instead of going by the coast we proceeded up the river, by the road leading to the rocks, and then continued under their shade till we reached the cascade, where we could cross, purposing to return by Family Bridge.

Our walk by the waterside proved most charming and agreeable. During the whole distance we enjoyed the pleasant shade from large trees in full foliage, or from the ridge of rocks which extended for a long distance between the beach and the stream. The soft grass under our feet formed a far more pleasant path than the pebbles and sand of the shore. Altogether the place was so attractive that my wife and I did not hurry ourselves, but sauntered along at our ease, while the boys rambled far and wide, and had got quite out of sight.

Before long, however, I saw them approaching at full gallop. Ernest arrived first, but gasping for breath, and unable for some time to utter a word.

'Papa!' he cried at last. 'Look! Potatoes!* We have found potatoes!'

'I am afraid,' I exclaimed, 'that news is too good to be true.'

The potato plant

* The potato plant is a native of South America. It was probably first brought into Spain from the neighbourhood of Quito in the 16th century. From Spain it found its way into Italy, and thence to Vienna. It appears to have been first introduced into Ireland from Virginia by Sir John Hawkins, a slave-trader, in 1565; and to England by Sir Francis Drake in 1585, but without attracting much notice, till it was a third time imported from Virginia by the colonists of Sir Walter Raleigh's expedition, who returned in 1586. Its first culture in Ireland is referred to Raleigh, who had large estates near Youghal, in the county of Cork. The potato is one of the most important of our cultivated food plants. The part eaten is not the root, but the tuber, a roundish body which is really a kind of underground stem, continuing a large quantity of starchy matter intended for the development of the stem and branches which spring from the buds on its surface and rise above ground. Potato starch, English arrowroot, and British gum or dextrine, are all made from the tuber.

'I think they *are* potatoes, papa,' said Fritz, somewhat confidently. 'Ernest has been very lucky to discover such a valuable treasure; there are acres of them.

'Let us go and see the spot,' I said. And with eager haste the boys led me to the place, and I was quickly convinced of the joyful fact that a little forest of potato-plants in full flower lay at our feet.

'Oh,' cried Jack, 'I knew they were potatoes! What a treat! If Ernest was the first to discover them, I will be the first to get you a supply.'

Accordingly he set to work to dig the roots up with his hands. Master Nip instantly followed his example; but he dug more quickly and cleverly than Jack, for he picked out the ripest; and in a very short time quite a large heap of potatoes had been gathered, from which we filled our sack and game-bags as full as possible.

Ernest proposed that we should at once return to Falcon's Nest, for two reasons – first, because the potatoes were a heavy load; and, secondly, that we might cook them for supper, and have a feast. But I reminded him that there existed still stronger reasons why we should go on, and we continued our walk pleasantly, and in good spirits, in spite of the heavy load.

At last a beautiful prospect lay before us, very different from anything we had hitherto seen. Tropical plants of all descriptions carpetted the ground – prickly shrubs, and flowers of every hue, which could only be reared in hothouses at home; the Indian fig;* the aloe,† crested with white blossoms; the tall,

* The Indian fig or prickly pear is a low plant, originally American, but now naturalised in Europe. It grows on the barest rocks, and has a fleshy stem, consisting of flattened joints (covered with sharp spines), inserted upon each other. Its fruit, which is oval, and about the size of a hen's egg, is of a yellowish colour, tinged with purple; the pulp, red and juicy, pleasantly combines sweetness with acidity. The plant lives in the south of England, and occasionally ripens there.

† The name aloe is the common name given to a large number of plants of the lily kind. They are especially abundant in the warm parts of Africa. Some of them are classed as trees and others as shrubs. From some of them the drug or

stately cactus,* with its prickly leaf and
amber flowers; creeping plants winding
their tendrils over every stem, and
spreading perfume around us from their
many-coloured blossoms. But, above all,
we were delighted to find fruit trees,
and among others, to our great joy, an
abundance of ananas or pineapples.†

I also discovered among the various
prickly-leaved plants a karatas,‡ a kind
of aloe, partly in bloom, but chiefly
covered with young shoots. This plant
was to me a welcome sight.

The aloe

'See, boys!' I called out. 'This is a most valuable discovery.
The under foliage of this plant resembles the pineapple; but the
stem is far more elegant. Observe how slender and upright it
grows and what beautiful red blossoms! I am glad to be able to
inform your mother that, when she wishes to mend our clothes,
I can now supply her with thread made from its filaments,' and I
explained that it was only necessary to dry the leaf in the sun, or
before the fire, in order to cause the fibres to easily separate
from their covering.

---

medicine aloes is obtained. It is the dried sap, got by cutting across the leaves.
The juice gathers on the outside, and is then collected.

* The cactus is the name given to a large number of plants of the Indian fig
order. They have fleshy stems (covered sometimes with hairs and sometimes
with spines) containing a milky juice. All the kinds, except one, are natives of
America. The Indian fig is a species of cactus.

† The pineapple, or *an-a'-na*, is a plant which belongs to South America and
the West Indies, but is now cultivated in all tropical countries. The fruit, which
has a delicious taste, something like, but much superior to, strawberries, varies
in size from $2^{1}/_{2}$ to 12 pounds in weight. Large quantities are sent to England
from the Bahamas. A kind of coarse cloth is sometimes made from the fibres of
the leaves.

‡ The karatas (*ka-ra'-tas*) is a plant found in great abundance in tropical
America and the West Indies. It is not of much commercial value.

The pineapple

The karatas and cactus

With this I split a leaf, and drew out a number of very strong yet beautifully fine threads, certainly not longer than the leaf, yet still long enough to form a needleful.

'You see, children,' I remarked to the boys, 'it is not safe to judge by appearances. The karatas, which you despised, proves far more useful than either the dainty pineapples or the potatoes. Its pith also supplies an excellent tinder.'

'Yes,' cried Ernest, 'I'll own it is very valuable, but what is the use of all the other prickly plants that grow in such profusion around us?'

'They are useful in many ways,' I replied, 'and some of them furnish the chief medicines used in Europe. The aloe, for example, is used to a very great extent in this way, and even these insects,' said I, pointing to a number of little brown creatures creeping and feeding on a species of prickly fig (with which Jack had wounded his hand in hastily snatching some fruit from the shrub) 'make the *cochineal** so much used at home.'

'But what is cochineal?' asked Ernest.

'A dye made from the small insects, that live on the leaf of this plant,' I answered. 'They are collected by people shaking them

Larva or grub of cochineal   *The cochineal insect*

* The cochineal insect is a kind of bug (about the size of a small ladybird), a native of the warmer parts of America, especially Mexico. It feeds on the cochineal fig, a species of cactus, very like the prickly pear. At a suitable time the females are gathered into a cloth by brushing the branches of the fig with the tail of a squirrel, or some other animal. The insects are killed by immersing them in boiling water, or by heating them in ovens. The dried bodies are then like small rough brown seeds, of which about 70,000 only weigh a pound. Crimson, scarlet, and carmine dyes are made from these dried bodies. The male insect is of no use for this purpose. Cochineal is one of the most important exports of Mexico.

from the trees into a cloth. When they are dried and packed together they form a very important article of commerce, as the richest and most beautiful scarlet dye is produced from them.'

While thus talking, we reached the shallow part of Jaguar River, and by crossing cautiously over the stepping stones, soon arrived at Tent House, which we found in the same state as when we left it.

Fritz ran to obtain a supply of powder and shot; my wife and little Frank hastened to fill a large jar which they had brought, with butter from the cask; while Ernest and Jack set off to the pond, and tried to catch the ducks and geese. But this was no easy matter, for the creatures had been living alone, and were quite wild. The boys found, at last, that to catch them they must use stratagem, and Ernest hit on the droll expedient of fishing for them with bait and line.

He had in his pocket a piece of cheese. This he broke into small portions, and tying a bit at the end of a long string, threw it into the water as bait. This was eagerly gobbled up by the greedy birds, and at last they were all drawn to land.

As we took the road back to Falcon's Nest, our little caravan presented a somewhat droll appearance; but the gaiety and gladness of our hearts caused us to forget the weight of our burdens; and we made no complaint.

Without delay, the boys prepared to light a fire for their mother to cook the longed-for potatoes; and when at length the much-praised and delicious supper was ready, we enjoyed it as much as we had anticipated. It was not without heartfelt thanks for the many mercies we enjoyed that we retired, fatigued and sleepy, to our castle in the air.

CHAPTER XIV

The Sledge

I had noticed the previous evening, as we came along the beach, a quantity of wood, which I thought suitable for making a sledge, on which to bring our casks and heavy stores from Tent House to Falcon's Nest. At dawn of day I woke Ernest, and, leaving the rest asleep, we descended. Then harnessing the ass to a strong forked branch of a tree that was lying near, we set off together to the shore. I had no difficulty in selecting suitable pieces of timber, which, having sawed to the right length, we tied together, and laid across the bough to which the ass was harnessed. Adding to the load a small sailor's chest, which we found half-buried in the sand, we returned homeward, Ernest leading the ass; while I followed, assisting to raise the load with a lever when we met with any obstacle. My wife had been somewhat alarmed at our absence; but seeing the result of our expedition, and hearing of the prospect of a sledge, she was well pleased at what we had done.

The chest was eagerly opened and examined. It was found to contain clothes and linen, almost completely spoiled by sea-water, but still of value to us.

Fritz and Jack had been shooting wood pigeons during our absence, and had consumed so much powder and shot that I felt it my duty to interfere; for at such a rate our store of ammunition would soon fail; and, besides, for the present, we had birds enough.

My wife agreed with this sensible advice, and I therefore showed them how to make snares for the birds from the threads of the karatas leaves. The two younger sons busied themselves with these, while I, with the elder boys, began to build the sledge. Whilst thus engaged, we heard a great commotion among our poultry. They screamed and cackled and fluttered about in such alarm, that we ran with all speed to the spot.

Quite by chance Ernest saw the monkey rush under one of the arched roots with a newly-laid egg in his paw, and disappear behind the tree as the boy approached. But Ernest was too quick for him; and, on searching, found the egg hidden in the grass with three others. We therefore decided to punish the young thief, by keeping him a prisoner every morning till the eggs were collected.

On returning to dinner, Jack, who had mounted into the tree to search for a suitable spot on which to place the bird-traps, came down hastily with the news that a pair of our pigeons were building a nest among the branches. I at once forbade all shooting in the trees, and decided that the idea of placing traps there for the birds must, for the present, be abandoned.

As the boys followed me to the spot at which I had left the wood, little Frank amused us by asking, 'Papa, why can't we sow gunpowder instead of those seeds? It would be much more useful than grain to us.'

His brothers laughed heartily, and Ernest exclaimed – 'Why, Franky, gunpowder is not a seed: it will not grow like oats!'

I then exclaimed to them that gunpowder is made of saltpetre, sulphur, and charcoal mixed together, and that Roger Bacon,* a monk, of Oxford, in England (who lived in the thirteenth century), discovered that these materials united would form an explosive substance.

---

* Roger Bacon was born at Ilchester, in Somerset, in 1214, and died at Oxford in 1292. He was one of the most wonderful men of his time. He made many valuable discoveries; that of magnifying glasses being, perhaps, the most important. Though the invention of gunpowder is commonly attributed to him, it appears to have been known to Berthold Schwartz, a monk of Goslar, south of Brunswick, in Germany, about 1320. Many writers maintain that it was known much earlier in various parts of the world, and some say that the Chinese and Hindus possessed it centuries before it was known in Europe.

By perseverance and hard work we managed to construct the sledge. I joined two curved pieces of wood by three pieces across, one in front and one behind, with a third in the middle. On these we nailed planks, and then, fastening the ropes to the outer points, the sledge stood complete.

My wife and the two young boys were occupied in plucking birds, while a number of them were already roasting before the fire on a spit formed from the blade of a Spanish sword (which belonged to one of the ship's officers). It seemed unnecessary to cook so many at once; but my wife explained that she was getting them ready for the butter-cask I was to bring for her on the new sledge, as she had decided to preserve them half-cooked and packed in butter, for use when other supplies should fail.

I prepared to start for Tent House with the sledge directly after dinner. In addition to arms, each of us carried, in our girdles of shark's skin, not only a hunting-knife, but a beautiful case, made by Fritz from his tiger-cat skin, containing a knife, fork, and spoon.

Fritz shooting wood pigeons

We harnessed both the cow and the ass to the sledge. Juno accompanied us, but Turk remained behind as a protection to those at home. Choosing the way by the sandy shore, we arrived without adventure at our storehouse.

We unharnessed the animals, leaving them to find pasture,

while we loaded the sledge, not only with the butter-cask, but also with the powder-barrel, the cask of cheese, and a variety of other articles. So engrossed were we in this work that we did not at first perceive that our two beasts, attracted by the fresh green turf, had wandered away across the bridge to the opposite shore, and had quite disappeared. I immediately dispatched Ernest in search of them with the dog, while I sought for myself a convenient spot in which to bathe, for the heat was very oppressive.

Wandering towards Safety Bay, I discovered a little creek, enclosed on one side by a marsh overgrown with magnificent reeds, and on the other by a chain of rocks stretching far into the sea; thus forming a most secluded bathing-place.

I called Ernest; but, as he did not make his appearance, I went to look for him, and was surprised at discovering the youngster lying at full-length, in a shady spot, sound asleep; while the ass and the cow which I had sent him to find were comfortably grazing beside him.

'Get up, you lazy fellow!' I exclaimed. 'Why, these animals might have recrossed the bridge, and given us a pretty chase!'

'No fear of that, papa!' he replied, as he lazily roused himself. 'I have removed a few planks from the end of the bridge, and it's not likely they will venture over it now.'

I bid him go and gather a bagful of the salt, which he had formerly noticed in the crevices of the rock, while I took my bath.

I found the sea most cool and refreshing, and dressed as quickly as possible after coming out of the water. Whilst I was cutting a bundle of reeds, suddenly I heard his voice exclaiming, 'Papa, papa, come quick! I have caught a huge fish! I can scarcely hold him!'

I ran immediately to his aid, and found him stretched upon the bank, and struggling with all his might to retain an enormous fish, whose efforts threatened to draw him into the water, line and all.

I quickly took the line from his hand, and lengthening it, to give the fish a little play, gradually drew it into a shallow. Ernest then waded into the water, and put an end to its struggles with a blow of his hatchet. I found it was a magnificent fish, apparently of the salmon kind, of about fifteen pounds weight, which would form a most excellent addition to our store of provisions, and be most acceptable to mother.

While Ernest had his bath, I cleaned and sprinkled the fish with salt; and then, harnessing the cattle to the sledge, we soon crossed the bridge and reached home without difficulty. At once I proceeded to display the contents of the sledge before the astonished eyes of our dear ones; and the butter and cheese casks, the reeds, the salt, and the fish were all greatly admired and praised.

After unloading, I fed the tired animals, adding some salt to their food, which they relished exceedingly, salt being as necessary to keep them in health, as for ourselves. We then sat down to a splendid supper of the fish caught by Ernest, and some baked potatoes. It was speedily finished, for we were wearied out; and retiring with thankful hearts to our hammocks, we were soon fast asleep.

CHAPTER XV

A Voyage to the Wreck – The Raft

Early on the following morning I announced a plan (which I had decided upon the previous day) of visiting the vessel, and requested Fritz to make preparations.

Collecting our arms and provisions, I called Ernest and Jack to give them some parting injunctions, but they were nowhere to be found. Their mother surmised they had gone to dig up a fresh supply of potatoes, and we therefore set out without waiting for their return, after saying a tearful farewell to mother and Frank.

Just as we reached the bridge at Jackal River, Jack and Ernest, to our astonishment, suddenly darted out from behind a bush, screaming and laughing over the trick they had played us. They begged that, as they had come so far, I would take them with me to the ship. I reproved them, and pointed out that this was impossible, for not only would they be too many for the boat, but those at home would be anxious at their nonappearance. I therefore ordered their immediate return, and was glad of the opportunity this gave me to send a message to my dear wife that we should remain all night, and she was not to feel uneasy on our account. Quickly embarking, we steered our little boat into the current which flowed into Safety Bay, and very soon reached the wreck.

Our first care was to collect suitable materials to construct a raft, which would carry more than our boat of tubs could hold. Choosing a number of empty barrels, we nailed them firmly together, and put a flooring of planks above, surrounding it with a railing about two feet high, thus succeeding in making a first-rate raft suitable for our purpose.

When it was finished we took a survey of the vessel, in order to decide what would be the most useful things to take back with us. It was now evening, and, after a comfortable meal, we retired to the captain's cabin, and slept soundly till broad daylight.

The next morning we set actively to work to load our two boats. After stripping the cabins, we took the locks from the doors, the bolts from the shutters, and all the furniture and fittings we could move. A couple of sea-chests belonging to the ship's officers proved a great prize; but of still greater value were the lockers of the ship's carpenter and the gunsmith.

The captain's trunk contained a valuable assortment of jewellery, consisting of gold and silver watches, chains, buckles, studs, and a snuffbox, most probably intended as presents, or as stock for profitable trade in a new colony, and a cashbox full of doubloons and piastres. But we were better pleased to find a number of young European fruit trees and plants, which had been most carefully packed for the voyage, and I recognised among them the pear, apple, orange, almond, peach, chestnut, and vine – fruit which in our dear native Swiss home we had so often enjoyed.

We discovered, also, a number of strong iron bars; a grindstone, a wagon, and cart wheels; a complete set of smith's tools, hatchets and shovels; chains, iron and copper wire; a ploughshare, a hand-mill, and not least important, several sacks full of maize, peas, oats, and other grain: in a word, a seemingly inexhaustible store of articles expressly provided for the support of a European colony to be founded in the Southern ocean. There were also parts of a sawmill, which we thought might be fitted together with little trouble, if we had strength enough to lift it, as the pieces were all numbered.

And now the question arose, which of all these valuable things should we take with us, and which leave behind?

I decided to take some powder and shot, iron, lead, and grain; together with the fruit trees and tools; and of these to place on the raft, and in our tub-boat, as much as we could possibly carry.

Among other things we had found a mariner's compass, and

two harpoons used in whale fishing, and Fritz begged me to fasten one of the latter to the bow of our little boat.

At length, when we were loaded with as much as could safely be carried, we fastened the raft to our tub-boat by ropes firmly attached at each corner, and, not without fear of disaster, we hoisted the sail and directed our course towards the shore. The wind assisted us, and we proceeded without meeting with the least impediment.

As we drew near the land, Fritz observed a strange-looking body moving on the waves, and asked me to examine it through the telescope. I soon recognised it to be a large turtle floating asleep on the surface of the water, and entirely unconscious of our approach.

As Fritz begged me to steer towards it, I complied with his desire; but the next moment a violent shock caused the boat to rock, while a noise as of a rope running through a reel was followed by a second shock and a rapid rushing forward of the boat.

'What is the matter, Fritz?' I exclaimed in alarm.

'I have him – I have him safe!' cried the youth eagerly; and I saw at once that my boy had really struck the turtle with the harpoon, and that the wounded animal, in its violent exertions to escape, was rapidly swimming and drawing the boat after it at a terrific speed.

I pulled down the sail immediately, and scrambled to the forepart of the boat, intending to cut the cord and set the turtle free, but Fritz stood ready with his hatchet and begged me to wait, assuring me there was no danger.

'I can cut the rope instantly, if it is necessary,' he said, and I yielded to his request, and returned to the helm.

Drawn by the turtle, we advanced rapidly, but as we drew near the shore I noticed that the creature was endeavouring to again reach the open sea. The wind blew landward, however, and I hoisted the sail; and at last we landed on a soft sloping shore not far from Falcon's Nest. Without delay I jumped into the shallow water, and despatched the turtle with my axe.

Fritz fired his gun to announce our arrival, and as usual all came to greet us. Great was their surprise, not only at the value of our cargo, but at the strange mode by which it had been brought into harbour.

While my wife and the boys went for the sledge on which to remove a part of our load, the rising tide carried the raft further up the beach, and on ebbing left it almost dry upon the sand.

The first article to be placed upon the sledge was the turtle. It was of enormous size, and weighed at least three hundredweight. To keep it in its place, we were obliged to pile around it the mattresses and other light articles which we had brought on shore. To assist the two animals in drawing their heavy load, each exerted all his strength, some pushing, others pulling, and so, in joyous procession, we set of for Falcon's Nest.

Our first care on arriving there was to unload the turtle, and lay him on his back, in order to remove the shell, and so get at the delicate flesh. Seizing a hatchet, with one blow on the breast of the animal, I separated a part of the shell, cutting off as much of the flesh with it as would serve for our supper. I advised my wife to cook it in the piece of shell, adding only a little salt. The head, the paws, and the entrails we gave to the dogs, and proceeded to salt the remainder.

'And the back of the shell,' cried Fritz – 'could we not make it into a water-trough? It would be so pleasant to have clean fresh water for our bath, or for washing our hands.'

'That would indeed be useful,' I replied, 'if your plan could be carried out. But we should require some clay with which to fix it in its place.'

'Oh, I can supply you with that,' exclaimed Jack, putting in his word. 'I brought some clay home this morning from the banks of the river.'

'When you have decided about the water-trough,' said Ernest, 'I will show you some white roots that I have discovered; our old sow eats them as if they were delicious. They appear to be a sort of horseradish.'

After examining them carefully, I replied, 'If I am not mistaken, my boy, you have made a most useful discovery. I believe this is the manioc* of which cassava-cakes are made by the inhabitants

*The manioc or
cassava plant*

of the West Indies. But it must be carefully prepared, for it contains a dangerous poison. However, it will provide us with a very palatable and nutritious substance, which we can use instead of bread. It is from this root that the well-known tapioca is made.'

While talking, we had been busily engaged in unloading the sledge, and, that task being now completed, I again set off with the three elder boys to bring another load from the boat before night set in. Frank remained behind to help his mother to prepare and cook the flesh of the turtle, so that when we returned, tired and hungry, we found a royal dish awaiting us.

We again loaded the sledge with as much as it would carry – the two chests, the wagon wheels, the handmill (which the discovery of the manioc

* The manioc (*man'-i-oc*), or cassava (*cā-sa'-vā*) plant is a native of tropical America, and is much cultivated there, as well as in Africa. Manioc is the Brazilian name, and cassava the West Indian one. It is a bushy plant, from six to eight feet high. The roots are turnip-like and more than a foot long. They sometimes weigh 30lb, and from three to eight generally grow in a cluster. All parts of the plant contain a burning milky juice, so poisonous as to cause death in few minutes; but this poison is dissipated by heat. The roots are grated down to a pulp, which is put into coarse, strong canvas bags, and submitted to pressure. The juice is thus squeezed out, and the starchy flour which remains is made into cakes and baked on hot iron plates. These cassava cakes form a valuable article of food, on which many of the inhabitants of Southern America live almost entirely. Under the name of Brazilian arrowroot the cassava meal is imported into England. Tapioca is also made from it. The meal, while moist, is heated on hot plates, and stirred about with an iron rod. This causes the starch grains to swell and burst, and to gather in small irregular lumps.

rendered doubly important and valuable to us), and as many of the smaller articles as we could find room for.

The supper of turtle proved most delicious; and when, after prayers, we ascended to our berths in the tree, and laid ourselves down on the blankets and mattresses brought from the ship (which we had hoisted up with our block and tackle), we quickly sank into a sweet and refreshing sleep.

CHAPTER XVI

Cassava Bread

At daybreak next morning, I got up without rousing any of the others, as I had my doubts about the safety of the raft and boat. Harnessing the ass to the sledge, I summoned the dogs, and went down to the beach. Both the boat and raft were quite safe, though the rising tide had changed their position; and, without delay, I placed upon the sledge a light load, and returned with it to Falcon's Nest. None of the family were awake, but at my call they soon appeared, somewhat ashamed of their indulgence, and after a hasty breakfast we repaired again to the shore; for I was anxious to have the boats unloaded before noon, that they might be ready to float as soon as the tide served.

By the time we reached Falcon's Nest with our last load, the tide had risen sufficiently, and I at once steered, with Fritz and Jack, to Safety Bay; for the beautiful weather, the calm sea, and the fresh breeze tempted me again to the wreck.

It was late in the day when we reached the vessel, and I merely collected what could be packed quickly and without much trouble. Jack found a wheelbarrow; and Fritz discovered something far more useful – the ship's pinnace,* carefully packed between decks, in pieces, all numbered, with rigging and fittings complete, and supplied with two small cannon. To raise the boat from its present position, fit it together and launch it, would require strength and skill, and I saw that it was impossible to commence such an undertaking now. I therefore directed the boys whilst they loaded the raft, urging them not to lose a moment. Among other useful articles we hastily put on board a

* A *pinnace* is a rather large boat, which may be propelled either by oars or sails, generally (but not always) provided with two masts.

copper boiler, a grindstone, two large iron plates, a powder cask, a box of flints for the guns (which were most welcome to me), several tobacco graters, and two more wheelbarrows beside Jack's. We again set sail; for I was anxious to avoid the land breeze, which generally rose after sunset.

My wife was delighted with our barrows (which we filled as full as possible with articles from our boat), but she looked rather doubtfully at the iron plates and the graters.

I warmly praised the industry of the two younger boys, who, during our absence, had collected a splendid store of potatoes, and a large number of manioc roots similar to those which Ernest had discovered on the previous day. As a reward, I gave each of them two of the smallest wheelbarrows for their own use.

The graters and iron plates were lying on the ground near us, and my wife, pointing to them, enquired, 'Of what use are these things, my dear?'

'They are to assist in providing you with fresh bread.'

'I cannot imagine,' she exclaimed, 'what tobacco graters have to do with new bread! Besides, even if you had flour, where is the baking oven?'

'Flat cakes can be baked upon these iron plates,' I replied. 'And, as for flour, that can be obtained from the cassava-roots. If you will make a couple of small strong bags of sailcloth, we will try an experiment in bread-baking before we sleep tonight.'

My wife soon got the bags ready; but I could see that she had not much faith in my powers as a baker, for she placed the newly-arrived copper boiler on the fire, filled with potatoes, to be ready for our supper in case the bread-baking should be a failure.

In the meantime I spread a large sailcloth on the ground, and set each of the boys to work with a grater and one of the carefully-washed manioc roots. In a short time we had a heap of what appeared to be moist white sawdust.

When a sufficient quantity had been scraped, I filled the bags and sewed up the ends tightly, so that when pressed only the poisonous sap might flow out between the threads of the cloth.

To obtain the means of pressing, I laid two or three smooth

planks on the table; and, placing the bags of flour upon it, covered them with another plank. I next took a long beam, and used it as a lever, by placing one end under the arched root of our tree; then heaping upon the other end lead, iron bars, and stones, with every heavy article I could find, the sap was very soon seen flowing to the ground below.

'I think we shall be able to commence bread-making soon,' exclaimed Fritz, after a time; 'not a drop of juice is falling from the bag now.'

'I am quite ready,' I replied; 'but, before we attempt to make bread for ourselves, a cake must be baked for the chickens and the monkey; if they eat it, and without harm, we may safely follow their example.'

The bag was opened and the meal spread out to dry. I moistened a small quantity with water, and adding a little salt kneaded it into a cake, which was laid on one of the iron plates over a clear fire made between large stones on the earth. As soon as the underside was brown, the cake was turned, and, when sufficiently baked, taken out to cool.

The cake exhaled such a delicious odour, that the boys looked with envy as I gave it to the animals; and had I not firmly opposed their longing, they would, I believe, have helped themselves.

I noticed with satisfaction that the fowls were eagerly eating up the crumbs, and that Master Nip was rapidly munching his piece of the cake with great gusto.

'See, my dear,' I said, addressing my wife, 'the animals have eaten it all, and we must begin our baking operations early tomorrow, if we find that our Nip and the fowls are not the worse for what they have eaten.'

We seated ourselves to partake of supper. The potatoes were excellent; and, once more with thankful hearts and appeased appetites, we retired to our castle in the tree.

CHAPTER XVII

The Pinnace

Finding next morning that the fowls and the monkey were as lively as ever, bread-baking for ourselves commenced in earnest. The boys were so proud of their performances that each ate his own cakes for breakfast; and a large bowl of new milk added to our meal made it a fit repast, luxurious enough for a king, whilst the poultry and pigeons came in for a share of the fragments.

During breakfast I expressed my strong desire to pay another visit to the wreck with the three elder boys, that we might, if possible, obtain possession of the pinnace which we had discovered on the previous day, for I was afraid the first change of wind might break up the wreck and we should lose it.

My dear wife could not be convinced, at first, that there was any necessity for me to venture again on the treacherous sea; but she at length consented, on condition that I would on no account remain another night on the wreck.

The boys were delighted, and to secure us against all ordinary risks, each of us was provided with one of the cork jackets which we had brought from the vessel on our previous voyage. Taking provisions for the day, we set sail in our tub-boat, having the raft in tow, and in due time reached the ship.

I directed the boys to load both the raft and the boat with the portable things that came first to hand, so that at least we might not return empty, whilst I hastened to examine the pinnace.

I discovered, to my great satisfaction, that as each piece of the vessel was carefully laid in its proper place and numbered, it could be put together with ease and correctness.

But so many difficulties presented themselves, that had it not been for the strong desire I felt to have in my possession such a beautiful little vessel, it is more than probable I should not have attempted the undertaking. I was convinced that, with patience and perseverance, we should be able to reconstruct the boat; and I determined to try and put it together, with the help of my boys, in the hope that some means for launching it would be suggested to me.

The evening set in before we had half effected our purpose, and we reluctantly returned home with our load. On reaching Safety Bay, we were delighted to see mother and little Frank on the shore waiting to receive us!' We have resolved to remain at Tent House,' said my wife, 'as long as you are visiting the wreck. It will be a shorter voyage for you, and we shall be constantly within sight of each other.'

I knew how little my brave wife liked residing at Tent House, and I failed not to thank her for this new token of her thoughtfulness. I was glad to be able to reward her self-denial by producing the things we had brought with us – two casks of salt butter, three of flour, some bags of wheat, rice, and other grain, with a large number of useful household articles and culinary utensils.

Next morning we returned to the ship; and an entire week was occupied with our voyages to the wreck. We started early every morning, and returned home in the evening, heavily laden, with such articles as seemed likely to be of the slightest use to us.

With incredible labour the pinnace was at last put together, and ready to be set free from her prison. Her appearance was neat and elegant. She had a tiller at her prow, and a small quarterdeck, on which to raise a mast and sail, like a cutter, and being of a light build would not draw much water. We carefully caulked all the joints and seams with pitch and tow, and on the quarterdeck we placed two small brass cannons, which we secured with chains in the usual manner on board ship.

But now the greatest difficulty remained. There sat the beautiful thing, immovable in its prison; and the thought that a storm might arise, and destroy both it and the wreck, led me to determine upon a most risky project, which I resolved to put into execution without saying a word to the boys.

I filled an old iron mortar (such as is used for pounding in by chemists), which we found in the steward's room, with gunpowder, and covered it securely with the end of a stout plank, in which I cut a groove and laid a train of gunpowder. Then, having contrived a fuse, which I thought would burn for an hour before reaching the powder, I closed every crevice with tar, and bound the whole together with chains and ropes to one of the largest bulkheads next the sea, on the side from which I calculated that the recoil of an explosion would set the pinnace free, yet without injuring it. Ordering the boys on board the tub-boat, I returned below deck, lighted the fuse, and hastily embarking, steered away from the wreck with a beating heart.

We reached the shore, and were unloading the raft, when a sudden and frightful noise on the sea, like thunder, made all stand aghast. My wife was the first to recover presence of mind.

'The sound seemed to come from the wreck!' she exclaimed. 'And look at the smoke! I hope, my dear husband, you have not left any fire near the powder!'

'There is nothing to fear,' I said. 'Boys, I must go back and see what has happened. Who will go with me?'

Without a word the three boys sprang into the boat, while I remained behind for a moment to whisper a word of explanation to my anxious wife, and to assure her there was no danger.

We quickly rowed out of the bay, and I saw with satisfaction that the side of the vessel nearest us remained unchanged. With a light heart I steered to the other side, and was amazed at the destruction caused by my petard. The greater portion of the ship's side had been shattered, and the fragments were floating on the water; while through the aperture we could see the pinnace, fully exposed to view, and uninjured.

'It is ours!' I cried in delight. 'The beautiful pinnace is ours!'

We climbed through the opening, and found, to our great delight, that with the aid of a pulley and lever we could push the pinnace from the wreck, for I had taken the precaution to place rollers under the keel.

Attaching a short cable to the head, and removing the timbers we had placed to keep it in position, we threw our united strength into the performance, and saw her glide slowly and

majestically into the sea. We wished to surprise mother and little
Frank with her wonderful appearance, so leaving her safe on the
side of the wreck farthest from the shore, we returned to Tent
House for the night, and explained that the explosion of some
gunpowder had injured the wreck, but that so many useful things
were left uninjured among the stores as to require us revisiting it
next day.

On returning in the morning, we found much to do. We got in
the mast and spars, put up the rigging and fully equipped our
elegant little vessel. This occupied us two days. We loaded the
craft with an ample cargo, including many articles too bulky for
our boat, and when all was ready we set sail. My boys obtained
permission, as a reward for their industry, to salute their mamma,
as we entered the bay, by firing our two guns. I acted as pilot.
Fritz was appointed captain, and Ernest and Jack, at his command, put their matches to the guns, and fired. My wife and
little boy rushed out in their alarm, but our joyful shouts
reassured them; and they were ready to welcome us with
astonishment and delight. Mooring the vessel at the landing-
place at the mouth of the river, Fritz placed a plank from the
pinnace to the shore, and assisted his mother to come on board.
They then fired a new salute, and christened the new vessel *The
Elizabeth*, after their dear mother.

Leaving our little fleet safely moored, we followed the river to
the cascade, where we saw a neat garden laid out in beds and
walks. 'We have not been idle: this is my work and Frank's,'
explained my wife. 'We found the earth soft enough for us to dig
and prepare. Here,' she continued, 'I have planted potatoes;
yonder are fresh cassava roots; on this side I have sowed lettuce,
cabbages, and other vegetables, and near them we have left a
space for you to plant a border of maize* and bamboo canes.'

---

* Maize, or Indian corn, is a kind of grass cultivated in almost all the warmer
parts of the world, where it answers a similar purpose to that of wheat in more
northern countries. The stem varies from two to eight feet in height. The ear,
or cob, is about a foot long, and a couple of inches thick, formed of grains

Leading us further on, and pointing to another division, she said, 'This will do nicely for our fruit garden, if you will plant here the fruit trees you found on the wreck; and yonder I have sowed a quantity of each sort of grain which you brought from the vessel. Water,' she added, 'can be easily brought from the neighbouring waterfall; and I have little doubt that the plants will grow and thrive, and we shall have a flourishing orchard.'

Head of maize, or corn cob

'You have performed wonders, dear wife,' I exclaimed, after examining the fruitful spot; and then, as the sunset was approaching, we unloaded our vessels, secured our pinnace to the shore by means of a rope from the bow, and loading the sledge with things for our immediate wants, we took the road to Falcon's Nest.

---

packed closely together. Maize is extensively cultivated in America, where it forms the chief bread food of many of the people. It is the most fattening of all the corn plants. Maize flour is called polenta, and maize starch is sold as cornflour, maizena, &c. The unripe grains are often roasted till they split, and are then called popcorn; prepared in this way they form a favourite food in the United States. The green stems and leaves form a nutritious food for cattle, and the plant is sown and cut green in this country for the same purpose.

CHAPTER XVIII

The Walk to Calabash Wood

I have always felt that it was our duty to make the lives of our young people as agreeable as possible, and to introduce such variety into their occupations as would prevent the 'daily round' becoming wearying and irksome.

After our midday meal, I therefore desired my boys to let me see their dexterity in such athletic sports as leaping, running, wrestling, and climbing, which, in addition to developing their bodily strength, would give them greater confidence in times of threatened danger. Nothing makes a man so timid and fearful as a want of confidence in his physical strength.

I also advised my boys to practice running up and down the rope-ladder that led to our room in the tree, and also to learn how to climb up a loose rope, which I suspended from a high branch. I made knots here and there in the rope at first; but after a little practice they managed to climb and descend with very few knots, and at last were able to go hand over hand with legs crossed, on a smooth rope and without assistance, as sailors do.

I next prepared for them another weapon, and proceeded to teach them its use. Tying a ball of lead to each end of a piece of rope about six feet long, I replied, in answer to their enquiries, that I was trying to make what is called a lasso, as used by the Mexicans and settlers in South America. Holding one end or the rope in the hand they swing the other end of it round or over their heads, and throw it with such power and swiftness that the animal they wish to capture is caught by the flying rope, which twists round its body and limbs, and renders it unable to move. 'The Mexicans,' I added, 'are so skilful with the lasso that they will throw it while riding on horseback at full speed, and they seldom fail in securing their prey alive, or in killing it.'

I made a trial of the lasso on the stump of a tree, and the rope wrapped itself so securely round it that the boys were more eager than ever to try the new weapon. Fritz speedily became skilful in throwing it, and I encouraged the rest to persevere in acquiring the same dexterity, as the weapon might be an invaluable resource when our ammunition failed.

The next morning I saw that the sea was too much agitated for any expedition in the boats, and we therefore determined to spend the day in home employments. We examined our stores for winter provision. My wife showed me a quantity of cakes of cassava-bread, carefully prepared. We also proceeded to plant the young fruit trees brought from Europe in the piece of ground my wife had selected for the purpose of an orchard.

The day wore away in these employments, and we determined to go next morning in pursuit of game to recruit our larder. At break of day we all started, taking with us the sledge, which contained our provision for the day, and on which we purposed to bring back any game we might secure. Turk formed the advanced guard; my sons followed with their guns; then came my wife with Francis leading the ass; and I closed the procession with Nip mounted on the patient Juno.

Passing through Flamingo Marsh, my wife and the younger boys, who had not seen the place before, were filled with admiration. Fritz, eager for some brilliant exploit, soon disappeared along with Turk, and we were presently startled by the noisy bark of the dog as an enormous bird rose in the air. A shot from Fritz brought it to the ground; but it was only slightly wounded, and with incredible strength it defended itself against both the dogs, for Juno, who could not look on, threw her little rider from her back to join in the chase.

Anxious to secure the bird (which was a fine bustard), without killing it, I threw my handkerchief over its head, tied its legs together, and released the wounded wing from the jaws of Juno. I wished to preserve it alive in the hope of taming it as an addition to our farmyard. We therefore bound it carefully and placed it on the sledge, and resumed our journey to the coconut wood, in which little Nip's mother had been killed by the dogs.

Ernest stopped suddenly as he espied the beautiful cluster of nuts which hung from the higher branches of a magnificent coconut palm. 'Oh, how terribly high the nuts are! I wish one would fall down!' he exclaimed.

Hardly had he uttered the words when, as if by magic, down dropped a nut at his feet. A second followed, much to our astonishment. 'Why, papa,' cried the boy, 'this is just like the fairy tale of the wishing cap. No sooner is a wish formed in the mind than it is granted.'

The boy cautiously picked up the nuts, and brought them to me. Presently two more fell, when Fritz cried out, 'See, papa, here comes the sorcerer. I have discovered him.'

Slowly and steadily a hideous creature glided down the trunk of the tree, but before it could reach the ground Jack struck at it with the butt-end of his gun. He missed his blow, however, and the animal, with gaping claws, advanced towards his assailant.

The little fellow defended himself bravely, but all his strokes failed to reach the animal. At last the boy stood still, took off his jacket, held it extended in both hands, advanced cautiously towards his adversary, and suddenly threw it over the animal; then, wrapping the jacket completely round the creature's body, I seized my hatchet, and with a few strokes killed the monster land-crab,* as I pronounced it to be.

Placing our prize on the sledge, I explained that the land-crab lives upon nuts, the shells of which he opens as much by skill as strength, perforating them through the holes at the narrow end of the nut, and that it is no mean adversity for a boy to meet and conquer.

* The land-crab is the popular name of all those species of crab which, in a natural state, do not live in the sea, but only visit it at the breeding season, in April and May, to deposit their eggs. They much resemble the common crab, and are remarkable as animals breathing by gills. They usually reside in the woods, and some of them burrow in the damp soil. The black mountain crab of the West Indies, which is the one here described, is chiefly active during the night. It lives almost entirely on vegetables, and is highly esteemed as an article of food. It is doubtful whether the stories told of its climbing the coconut trees for the purpose of obtaining the nuts are quite true.

We proceeded on our journey very slowly on account of a thick growth of tall grass and underwood and the tendrils of creeping plants. At times we had to stop, and with our axes cut a way for the sledge, but, after pushing on for some distance through the thicket, we came to a clearing, and saw before us, near the seashore, the beautiful calabash trees,† forming a delightful shelter. The splendid trees and their singular fruit excited both wonder and surprise. Whilst explaining to my boys the varied forms of the gourds, we set to work immediately to make from them a good supply of such household vessels as we needed, viz., flasks, bowls, and plates, for the ones we had made in our previous expedition were, by this time, almost all worn out.

Being fatigued with our work, we sat down under the shade of the trees and took some refreshment. Ernest, with his brothers, then set off to search for water and to explore the wood. Suddenly we saw him running to us in great terror, shouting, 'A wild boar, papa! a wild boar!' Fritz and I seized our guns, and, with the dogs, ran to the spot he pointed out.

We heard barking and loud grunting as though a combat had begun, and hoping for a good prize we hastened forward. But to our amazement we found the dogs holding by the ears, not a wild boar, but our own sow, whose wayward and intractable disposition had caused her to leave us and live in the woods! We could not but laugh at our alarm, and calling off the dogs I released the poor sow, who immediately resumed her feast on a species of apples, which appeared to have fallen from the trees. I picked up one of them, and found it to resemble a medlar, rich

† The calabash tree is the popular name of an American tree which grows about 30 feet high, with narrow clustered leaves and variegated flowers. The fruit, called gourds, is globular or oral-shaped (considerably larger than a coconut), the woody shells of which, when dried, are applied to many useful household purposes, being so hard and close-grained that when they contain liquid they may be put several times on the fire as kettles. The tree grows abundantly in tropical America and the West Indies. The pulpy inside of the shell is not of much use.

and juicy in flavour, but did not venture to taste it till we had put it to the usual test. We collected a quantity, and I also broke off a loaded branch from the tree. On presenting one to Nip he ate it with great relish. Satisfied with this test, I examined the fruit more carefully, and decided that it must be the guava,* a luscious South American fruit; we therefore ate some ourselves, and found them pleasant and refreshing.

Jack, who had set off with his gun, had scrambled through a

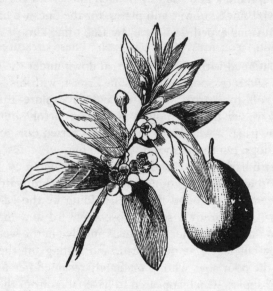

The guava

---

* The guava (*gwâ'-vă*) is a species of myrtle tree rarely exceeding 20 feet in height. It is a native both of the East and West Indies, though it is not improbable it was introduced into the East Indies from tropical America. The fruit, which is about the size of a hen's egg, is of an agreeable flavour. A delicious jelly, called guava jelly, is made from it, and is largely exported to England from the West Indies. There are two chief species, the red and white guava. The latter is the one here meant.

thicket and up a rocky mound at a little distance; but no sooner had he reached the summit than he stood still with a horror-stricken face, as if unable to move, and exclaimed, 'Papa, papa, a crocodile, a crocodile!'

I was inclined to smile at his simplicity, knowing that such a monstrous reptile was not likely to be found in so unsuitable a locality. 'A crocodile!' I replied. 'So far from the water as this? That would indeed be singular.' However, we all rushed to the spot, and I immediately recognised a large lizard, named the iguana,* the eggs and flesh of which are much esteemed as delicious eating in the West Indies.

Fritz raised his gun to fire, but I checked him. 'Steady, my boy,' I said. 'You must not be so rash. These creatures have a wonderful tenacity of life, and we must use other means to capture our booty.'

I cut a strong stick, and fastened a string to the end of it with a slipknot. In my left hand I carried a slight switch, and slowly approaching the sleeping creature, I whistled softly as I drew nearer. The animal presently awoke, and raised his head to listen. I advanced with caution until near enough to pass my slipknot round his neck, still continuing to whistle, and made him captive with ease. I dragged him to the foot of the rock, turned him over on his back, and forthwith despatched him.

We could not think of leaving such a valuable prize behind us, and as our sledge was a long way off, I resolved to carry the creature on my back. The boys followed to support the tail, for the weight was enormous, and laughed immoderately at the ludicrous figure I presented with my unusual load.

We chose the shortest way back; but long before we reached Frank and his mother, our long absence had alarmed them. All

* The iguana (ĭg-wâ'-nă) is a lizard-like reptile, with a long tail, very timid and nimble, which is abundant in the West Indies and tropical America, living mostly among trees. It attains a length of about five feet, and is of a greyish-yellow colour, mottled with green. Its flesh is considered a great delicacy, and its eggs (which are about the size of those of a pigeon, but without a hard shell, and are laid in the sand) are also eaten.

The sleeping iguana

trouble was, however, speedily forgotten when we began to recount our adventure; for many questions were asked, and much had to be related; but it was already growing late, and we began to feel hungry.

As it was quite impossible to prepare a piece of the iguana for dinner, we were obliged to content ourselves with the cold provisions we had brought with us. I readily gave the boys permission to eat some of the guavas, and never, I believe, was fruit so thoroughly enjoyed. It was so full of juice that it supplied the place of water, and our thirst was thereby relieved.

Refreshed and strengthened, my wife proposed that we should prepare to turn our steps homeward, and I readily agreed to her suggestion.

We started for Falcon's Nest, and presently entered a wood of majestic evergreen oaks,* beneath which lay a quantity of acorns, on which the bustard fed with great eagerness. Before night set in we were at home; and a piece of iguana's flesh, baked with potatoes, formed our supper, after which, with thankful hearts, we retired to rest in our aërial dormitory, and slept soundly till morning.

---

* The evergreen oak, also called the holm oak, is a native of the south of Europe and the north of Africa. It is a very ornamental tree, and its wood is exceedingly hard and durable. The acorns are sometimes bitter and sometimes sweet. In the latter case they are often eaten.

CHAPTER XIX

Another Exploring Expedition

Early next morning Fritz and I started to bring home the sledge. On arriving at the wood of evergreen oaks, we found our sow busily regaling herself on the acorns. She was none the worse for her encounter of the previous day, and not in the least shy or wild.

While passing through the wood, we observed a variety of beautiful birds, several of which especially excited my curiosity. Fritz earnestly requested permission to fire at them, and although I most strongly objected to all needless destruction of life in mere thoughtlessness or for sport, I at last gave consent, in order that we might ascertain their species, and see if any of them would be useful for food. A single shot brought down three of them, two parrots and a great Virginian jay.

Placing our prizes on the back of the ass, we continued our journey. At last we arrived at the guava trees, and after refreshing ourselves with some of their fruit, we proceeded to the spot where we had left the sledge.

As the day was yet early, I determined to carry out a plan I had long had in my mind, of making a further exploration. Taking the ass with us to carry provisions, we hastened towards the chain of rocks, Turk leading the way. My intention was to discover, if possible, whether we were on the inner side of an extensive promontory or on an island. (I may here mention that we afterwards found we were living on a large island, apparently not far from the mouth of some mighty river.*)

* In the original edition this island was located near New Guinea; but an island in tropical America, situated between the mouths of the Amazon and the Orinoco, would more fitly correspond with the incidents narrated, and their surroundings.

We first passed a small brook, then large tracts of land covered with manioc and potatoes, and finally reached a grove of bushes, from the branches of which hung curious clusters of white berries exactly like wax. We picked several, and found that the warmth of our hands made them stick to our fingers. I pronounced them to be the curious fruit of the candleberry myrtle† or wax tree.

'Are they of any use, papa?' asked Fritz.

The candleberry or wax myrtle

'They are of no use as food; but we shall be able to make candles from them for our winter evenings.' This prospect

---

† The candleberry or wax myrtle is a common shrub in North America, growing to about 14 feet high. The berries are the size of peppercorns, and covered with a greenish-white wax (popularly called bayberry tallow). A bushel of berries yields four to five pounds of wax. This is a different tree to the wax palm of the Andes.

greatly pleased Fritz; and he readily assisted me in filling a bag with berries for the ass to carry home.

As we continued our journey, our conversation turned on the sociability of birds, and the skill displayed by them in building their nests. Fritz asked if there were other creatures with similar powers and habits, and whether the architectural skill they displayed was the result of instinct or of reason – a difficult question to answer.

'Beavers,' I replied, 'build quite a village on the banks of rivers, in which large numbers live together in communities. By their united efforts they construct dams across streams of great size. Bees, wasps, and ants, also, have this social instinct strongly developed.'

Thus conversing, we reached a wood containing some trees quite unknown to us. They were apparently from forty to sixty feet in height, and from the bark, which was cracked and scaled in some places like that of the pine, issued small balls of thick gum. It was with difficulty Fritz gathered some of them. He tried to soften it with his hand as we continued our walk, but found that heat only gave it the power of extension, and that on being released it returned again to its original form.

'Look, papa!' he exclaimed, pointing to a cluster of tall trees, 'I believe these are caoutchouc trees,* and that this is indiarubber.'

'That would be indeed a valuable discovery,' I replied.

'Why, what use can be made of indiarubber except to remove pencil-marks?'

'The sap of the caoutchouc tree,' I answered, 'will be of great

* Caoutchouc (*coo'-tchook*) or indiarubber is the solidified, milky, resinous juice of several tropical plants and trees; the largest supplies being obtained from Assam and Java, in Asia, and Guiana and Brazil in South America, especially from the latter. It was first brought to Europe about 1735, and its property of rubbing out lead pencil marks was noticed by Dr Priestly, of Leeds, in 1770. Immense quantities of the article are now used in commerce and the arts, especially since the discovery, in 1839, of a method of combining it with sulphur, which prevents it hardening by cold, becoming sticky by heat, and dissolving in grease and oil. Thus prepared it is called vulcanised indiarubber.

The indiarubber tree

service to us. From this gum we shall be able to make bottles, and many useful articles – and, besides, I have a plan in view for shoemaking!' I explained to Fritz further, how the milky resinous juice, which flows from the trees in considerable quantity when they are properly tapped, is formed by the natives of Brazil, Guiana, and Cayenne into the bottle rubber of commerce.

By this time we had reached the coconut wood, and it occurred to me to look for some of those most valuable trees called the sago palm.* I noticed, after a time, a large tree broken down by the wind. The centre of the trunk was quite full of a white dust, of a floury nature, exactly resembling European sago. A grove of sugar-canes lay in our homeward way, and, not to return empty-handed, we added a large bundle of them to our patient ass's load.

* Sago in a kind of starch. It is the cellular substance formed in the centre of the stem (not properly the pith, though often called so) of several kinds of palm trees. The tree from which the finest sago is obtained forms immense forests on nearly all the Moluccas – a group of islands, often called the Spice Islands, in the Indian Archipelago, between Celebes and New Guinea – and in Sumatra. Each tree, which yields from 100 to 800lb of sago, grows to a height of 30 feet, and from 12 to 22 inches in diameter. The trees are cut down just before they flower, and the centre part is grated into powder, like sawdust, and washed in water. The starch settles to the bottom of the vessel, and is afterwards dried, and by a mechanical process rubbed into small grains. Sago is first sent to Singapore to be purified and made ready for the market, from whence it is re-exported.

CHAPTER XX

Candle-Making

When the boys rose next morning they gave me no rest till I promised to attempt to make candles of the wax-plant berries.

We first filled a pan (which was one of the treasures saved from the wreck) with the berries, and placed it over the fire. In a little time a considerable quantity of beautiful green wax was produced. This I carefully skimmed off into another vessel, and while the berries were melting we prepared a number of wicks from threads of sailcloth. These we dipped quickly and carefully into the wax, and then hung them in the air to harden. This operation was repeated several times, till the wicks had taken sufficient wax to form candles. The same evening, one of them was placed in a clay socket and lighted on our supper table, and although they were far inferior in roundness and size to those at home, they threw around us such a clear, bright light, that we were overjoyed with the result.

Our success in this important matter encouraged me to make an attempt of another description. Among the articles on board ship we found no churn, and I therefore resolved to try a plan which I remembered was practised by the Hottentots, who make butter by shaking cream in a skin.

I chose the largest of our gourd bottles, and filled it half full of cream, closing it tightly. I next placed four stakes firmly in the ground, tied to them a piece of sailcloth by the four corners, and laid the bottle upon it. At each of the four sides I placed one of the boys, and directed them to roll the vessel backwards and forwards, by alternately raising the cloth in pairs, so as to keep it in constant motion. This employment proved capital fun; and the boys kept it up with great mirth and laughter for more than half an hour. I then opened the bottle, and found, to our great joy, that some really good butter had been churned.

My next work was a much more difficult undertaking, and for a long time it seemed impracticable. The sledge was not only inconvenient but very heavy for our animals to draw; but as we had brought four cart wheels from the wreck, I determined to try and construct a little cart, and after some difficulty succeeded in building a sort of carriage, which, though clumsy in appearance, would, I knew, be very useful.

While I was thus employed my wife and some of the boys went daily to Tent House to plant the European seeds which I had brought from the wreck. As I wished also to make the rocks at Tent House a kind of fortification (for all our ammunition lay there), I resolved to choose two slight elevations near the river, on which to fix the two cannon from the pinnace, and also to plant a thick hedge of Indian fig and other thorny plants of the cactus kind around the whole spot.

These operations employed us day by day for six weeks; but the hard work had completely worn out our clothes, for our wardrobe was scanty; and this, with other reasons, made me consider it advisable to return once more to the wreck. I wished, if possible, to bring away some large chests, and one or two more of the cannon to place on the heights of our fortification.

Accordingly, on the first fine day, I set out in the pinnace for the wreck with the three elder boys. We found everything almost as we had left it; but the wind and waves had done considerable damage. The sailors' chests were in fairly good condition, and these we placed on board the pinnace, as well as a quantity of powder and shot, and two small cannon.

On our next trip we towed our tub boat behind the pinnace, and loaded it with planks, doors, window-shutters, locks and bolts, and as many other valuable things as we could possibly carry. In fact, we plundered the wreck of every useful article, and I then resolved to blow the hull up with gunpowder, in the hope that the wind and the waves would cast on shore planks and beams (as well as other articles suitable for house building), which were too bulky for us to move or bring away in our boats. I had noticed four large copper cauldrons, which I thought might be saved, and as they were too heavy to move, I attached to them several empty casks strong enough to support them when the ship broke up.

When all was ready for our last voyage home I placed a barrel of powder in the hold of the ship, fastened a fuse to it carefully, and lighting it, sprang into the boat. The boys were already seated, and with outspread sail we made towards the shore.

We had scarcely reached Safety Bay when a mighty roar as of thunder resounded from the rocks, and at the same moment a brilliant column of fire and smoke, shooting into the air, announced that my plan had succeeded. A feeling of sadness came over us all. It seemed as if the last link that bound us to our dear home was broken, and that we had lost in the ship an old and trusted friend.

Refreshed by a night's rest, which enabled us to shake off all feelings of regret, we hastened to the shore, when we saw that the beach was strewn with planks and beams; whilst on the sea, but rather beyond our reach, floated broken fragments of all descriptions, and amongst them the copper cauldrons, buoyed up between the casks to which I had fastened them. Many days were employed in collecting all these useful articles, in piling them on the shore, and in placing the powder casks under the cauldrons, covering them with earth and moss, till we could store them properly at Tent House.

My wife, after assisting us with the wreckage, made the agreeable discovery that two of our ducks and one of the geese had each hatched a brood, and she had seen them leading their noisy young families to the water. This reminded us of our domestic comforts at Falcon's Nest, and we determined to leave the next morning for our shady summer home.

CHAPTER XXI

Another Excursion

On our way to Falcon's Nest I observed that the newly-planted fruit trees were beginning to droop for want of supports, and I resolved, therefore, to proceed to Cape Disappointment the next day, to cut a supply of bamboos for props. We took the cart, harnessing both the ass and the cow to it, and started in high spirits. As soon as the candleberry trees came in sight the boys rushed off and eagerly gathered berries enough to fill two sacks, which were stowed away safely in a spot we should pass on our way home.

When we reached the caoutchouc trees I at once made several incisions in the bark, through which the sticky, whitish gum oozed, though not at first very freely.

In order to catch the drops, we fixed under the gashes several gourd vessels (which we had brought for the purpose), leaving them to be collected on our homeward journey, and then continued our route till we reached the coconut wood.

Presently we arrived at an open spot situated between the grove of sugar-canes and the bamboo bushes, which lay at a little distance beyond. Here we paused to admire the beautiful landscape which lay stretched out before us. On our left was the sugar-cane grove, to the right the bamboos, behind us a splendid avenue of palm trees, and in front the great bay, with Cape Disappointment extending far out into the deep sea.

The great beauty of the scene made us feel inclined to remove from Falcon's Nest, and take up our abode here; but the safety of our dwelling in the great tree, and the labour we had expended on it, with other advantages which we enjoyed there, made us decide to remain at the dear old home.

We determined, however, to make a halt for the night. The

Climbing the palm trees

animals were quickly unharnessed from the cart, and set at liberty to graze on the rich and luxuriant herbage which grew beneath the palms. Then all set to work to cut down and tie together bamboo and sugar-canes, in suitable bundles for placing on the cart. The boys cast many longing eyes on the coconuts, and at last Fritz and Jack attempted to climb the tree; but the trunk was too large and too smooth for them, affording no resting place or prop to aid their efforts, and they slid to the ground again.

In this dilemma I produced some rough pieces of the shark's skin which I had put in the cart on purpose, and, after fastening them tightly to their arms and knees, told them to try again, as the rough surface would enable them to rest and take breath while clinging to the stern with their knees.

Fritz and Jack made the attempt, and with these helps soon reached the crown of the tree. Each took an axe from his leathern girdle and struck so bravely at the clusters of coconuts that we soon had a plentiful supply of them. The boys were almost beside themselves with delight, and on coming down received our congratulations that this gymnastic performance had been so successful.

Ernest, who thus far had been inactive, was soon seen climbing a tree on which no fruit grew. In response to a laugh from his brother, he took his axe from his girdle, and with one or two strokes cut off several tufts of the large, delicately-formed yellow leaves from the crown. 'See,' he cried, 'I have thrown down something twenty times more agreeable to eat than coconuts. This tree, I am sure, is the cabbage palm.'*

'Bravo!' I exclaimed, as I examined a leaf, 'you are quite right, and very wholesome food it is.' Ernest had asked the loan of a

* The cabbage palm is a native of Jamaica and the West Indies. It is one of the most graceful of this class of trees, having a stem of about 20 inches in circumference, which often rises to a height of above 150 feet. It is crowned by a large head of leaves, in the centre of which grows a single bud of unopened leaves, which is much prized as a vegetable. The removal of this bud completely destroys the tree.

coconut shell from his mother before going up, and when he descended to the ground, he produced the shell, which he presented to me, saying, 'See, father, this is palm wine.'

'You are right,' I replied. 'We will all drink to your health, and to the success of your discovery.'

The sun was now sinking in the west, and we set to work to pitch our tent for the night, and to build a little cabin. I had brought a piece of sailcloth, which we used as a covering to our little hut, and to protect us from the night air.

While thus occupied we were startled by the extraordinary behaviour of the ass. He was quietly grazing near us, when suddenly he began to toss his head in the air as if he were in the midst of fire and flame, then, uttering a loud bray, he started off at full gallop, and disappeared among the bamboo bushes. Summoning the dogs, we cautiously followed him for some distance, but with no success, and were reluctantly compelled to defer further search till the morrow.

This circumstance alarmed me, and I could only account for the poor animal's excitement by the probable approach of wild beasts. To guard against all danger, therefore, I determined that large fires should be lighted with dry reeds to surround our hut.

We laid ourselves down on the soft beds of grass and moss, which the boys had collected, with loaded guns close at hand in case of danger. For a long time I kept awake to replenish the fire, but as no wild beasts appeared I gradually sank into a refreshing sleep.

During breakfast next morning we laid our plans for the day. I had hoped our donkey would have returned, but as no traces of the wanderer appeared, I resolved to take Jack and the two dogs, and search for the fugitive, returning to the hut before evening.

With the help of the dogs, we were able to follow the donkey's tracks through the canebrake, and at length emerged on the shores of a large bay.

We climbed the lofty cliffs, and found on the other side, to the left, a large river, which overflowed its banks. Its bed was deep, and the rush of its waters so rapid, that we found with difficulty a place where we could safely ford it. I saw with pleasure the print of many hoofs on both banks, but soon all trace of this trail was lost in the grass. I now became anxious to reach home, and as it was too late to search further we set off on our return.

Halting for a short rest, I recognised a small tree as the dwarf palm, whose long sharp leaves form an excellent barrier if it is planted as a hedge. I determined to return at the first opportunity, and get some young plants to strengthen our hedge at Tent House.

We readily found our way back again to the road; but night was approaching before we reached the palm grove, where we were received with shouts of joy. Question after question had to be answered, and Jack described our adventures in so spirited a manner, and was listened to with such eager curiosity, that I had scarcely time before supper to ask what my dear ones had all been doing in our absence.

The Malabar eagle

They informed me at last that they had visited Cape Disappointment, gathered wood for the night, and cut down a large palm, which they believed to be the sago palm. Fritz had discovered a young Malabar eagle.* As these birds are easily tamed, he hoped to train him to bring down birds in the chase like a falcon.

During their absence, however, the hut had been invaded by a troop of monkeys. They had drunk up all the palm wine from the calabash bowls, scattered the potatoes, stolen the coconuts, and so damaged the building that my young people, on their return, were several hours employed in repairing it.

Jack and I were both weary with our day's labour, and were thankful to stretch our tired limbs on the soft dried grass and moss in the tent, where we slept soundly and undisturbed till sunrise.

---

* The Malabar or *Chee'-la* eagle is a native of India, and is capable of being trained for the chase like a falcon.

CHAPTER XXII

Various Manufactures and Improvements

At daybreak all were astir, refreshed with a night's rest, to undergo the fatigues of another day. After a light breakfast I gave the signal to prepare for a return to Falcon's Nest, when I observed that my young people had some project in their heads which rendered them unwilling to leave so early.

'What is all this whispering about?' I asked of my wife.

'The boys,' she replied, 'are anxious to remove the inner part of the fallen sago palm before it is spoiled; and Fritz fancies we could make of the trunk two pipes to conduct the water from Jackal Bay to Tent House. This would enable us to water our plants in the dry weather, and would be a great advantage to us.'

This suggestion pleased me greatly, and we made ready to carry it out; but the work required patience as well as activity, and with all our efforts we could not get the task completed till sunset. It was necessary, therefore, to remain for another night in our tent. On the following morning we rose early, collected our treasures together, and without loss of time made preparations for carrying our newly-acquired possessions to Falcon's Nest.

We passed the places where we had left the sack of wax berries and the calabash cups containing the gum from the indiarubber trees. These we stowed away in the cart, and resuming our journey, I sent Fritz and Jack on before with one of the dogs. They went quickly forward and entered the guava grove at a little distance in advance of us.

A most terrible noise suddenly reached our ears, which, with the violent barking of the dogs, caused great alarm. Dreading the attack of some fierce animal, I made ready my gun, flew to the assistance of my children, and was about to fire, but on arriving at the spot, there was Jack, lying at full length on the ground between the shrubs, ready to burst with laughter. On seeing me he exclaimed, 'Oh, papa, how absurd! It is our old sow again: she must play these tricks on us on purpose. Just look here!' Half inclined to be angry and half amused, I heard the familiar grunting, and stepped among the bushes. There, sure enough, lay our sow, looking very happy, with seven lively little pigs seemingly only a few days old. We left with her some potatoes, acorns, and biscuit, and, continuing our journey reached home, as we now called Falcon's Nest, without further interruption.

The next morning I rose early with the intention of carrying out the project so long decided upon, namely, the planting of bamboo canes as a support to the young trees on the road to Tent House. Our work began almost as soon as we left Falcon's Nest, at the entrance to the road to Tent House, with the walnut, chestnut, and cherry trees. These had been planted in rows, and they were already much bent and curved by the wind.

Whilst we were hard at work our conversation naturally turned upon the best manner of raising trees, and the boys overwhelmed me with questions.

I explained to them that many of the most valuable fruit trees of Northern Europe grow without cultivation in the south of Europe and Asia, and others in more distant parts of the world. Crab-apples, for instance, grew wild in England in the time of the Romans, and in that country no other fruit was then known but common nuts, crab-apples, and blackberries. By grafting from foreign trees on the crab-apple, and also on the common nut and blackberry, most of the delicious apples, filberts, strawberries, and raspberries have been produced.

'Can you tell us, papa,' asked Ernest, 'where all the different fruit trees came from?'

'I think I can give you the history of a few trees. Walnuts came originally from Persia, and hazel nuts from Pontus, in Asia.'

'But cherries, papa?' interrupted Jack. 'I hope they are natives of Europe.'

'No, my boy,' I replied. 'They also have been brought from

other lands. They are named cherries after Cerasus,* a state of Pontus, in Asia, from which place they are said to have been first carried to Rome by Lucullus, a Roman general, who lived about seventy years before Christ.'

At noon we returned to Falcon's Nest, as hungry as hunters, just as my dear wife had prepared for us a most excellent dinner, consisting chiefly of the cabbage palm. We dined with good appetites, and, while resting, I took the opportunity of speaking on a subject which, for a considerable time, had occupied my mind.

We had often found it difficult to mount to our sleeping chamber by the rope ladder. Accidents so easily happen, and a single false step might cause a fall. It seemed to me that a wooden staircase might be contrived in the interior of the large trunk of our tree, if only it was hollow.

'Did you not tell me, wife,' I said, 'that in the trunk of this tree you had discovered a hole through which bees were passing?'

'Yes,' she replied; 'and it is evidently hollow beyond the point at which I have seen the bees enter. If hollow to the foot of the tree it will help you greatly to carry out your project.'

This idea of a staircase so excited the boys that they danced about the tree, and climbed like squirrels as high as they could reach, to discover from the sound produced by knocking against the trunk with axe and hammer, how far down the cavity extended. But this daring performance cost them dearly. The noise so disturbed the bees that a swarm of them rushed out, and furiously attacked the children with their stings.

I at once determined to remove the bees from the tree. My first care was to make for them a new hive, and, taking a large gourd, I flattened the lower half, so that, when finished, it might stand firmly on a piece of board nailed to a branch of the tree. I then cut a small opening in front for a doorway, and made a straw roof to place over it as a protection against sunshine and rain. This work occupied more time than I had anticipated.

---

* (Pronounced *sĕr'-ă-sŭs*, not *sĕr-ā'-sŭs*.) This derivation of the name is now considered doubtful, as the town probably received its name from the fruit.

I was therefore obliged to put off the assault on the bees till the next morning.

The impatience of the young people roused us all at an early hour, and I began my undertaking by stopping up the hole in the tree, through which the bees passed in and out, with moist clay, only leaving room to insert a piece of hollow cane, which was to serve as a tobacco-pipe. I then covered my head with a piece of linen, and began puffing tobacco smoke into the nest.

After a while, when all was still, Fritz climbed to my side, and with chisel and axe, he cut away a portion of the tree, about three feet square, while I continued smoking both inside and outside the tree till the bees were stupefied. The piece of the tree which had been cut away was then removed, and when the light entered I discovered that the whole trunk was hollow as high as the floor of our sleeping chamber. It was clear that we could build a winding staircase inside it with ease.

We were filled with delight at the beautiful work of the bees, and could scarcely find basins and bowls for so large a supply of honey and wax. I placed the bees in their new hive, and as the queen bee had fortunately been removed with them, they settled quietly, after a while, in their new habitation.

Without losing time we set to work on our staircase. With the help of my boys I cleared away all the decayed wood that remained in the hollow trunk of the tree, and carefully cleaned the sides of the interior as far up as we could reach. In the centre was placed upright, and firmly fixed in the ground, a strong palm tree stem, about a foot in thickness and of sufficient height. Around this I fixed the steps, formed of barrel staves, in the form of a spiral, to grooves cut in the side of the tree. The entrance of the tree, which I had enlarged, gave us sufficient light for our work. To this opening we added a second one, as the steps rose higher, and even a third one, to enable us to reach our sleeping room above without the trouble of climbing our rope ladder. A long rope was now fastened outside the steps instead of a bannister, for us to hold by as we ascended and descended. My winding stairs was then complete, and if not exactly in accordance with the rules of architecture it was yet solid and convenient. We thought it superb.

We did not, however, work uninterruptedly at this improvement to our house, nor in such a way as to make our work an oppressive toil. Various domestic incidents and different occupations relieved us from time to time, and diversified our proceedings. Among other wants that had to be supplied, candle-making was very urgent, as our present store, which had lasted a long time, was nearly exhausted. But a great difficulty arose; for my dear Elizabeth, like a prudent housewife, objected to the use of our handkerchiefs and cotton neckties for wicks. I attempted to supply the place with thin strips of touchwood, and at my wife's suggestion tried to make use of the threads of the karatas leaves; but after repeated experiments the decision was, for the present, in favour of the cotton wicks, much as we might wish to dispense with them.

After making a store of candles I tried my skill in the manufacture of indiarubber shoes from the sap of the caoutchouc tree.

First filling a pair of my stockings with sand, I covered them with a very thin coating of clay, which was quickly dried in the sun. Then, with a brush made of goat's hair, I laid on three coats of the melted caoutchouc to obtain a proper thickness, and hung the shoes in the sun to dry and harden.

After an hour or two the caoutchouc had solidified, and when I threw out the sand and removed first the stocking and then the clay, a pair of boots, so useful and shapely, was the result, that my boys begged me to make each of them a pair of the same sort. In time I supplied all the family with foot covering, not altogether elegant in shape, but most useful.

One thing I was most anxious to do at once, for the children often grew tired of drawing water from the river for our domestic use, as they had to carry it a considerable distance. By lengthening the sago-palm trunks, which we had made into channels to conduct water from the bay to Tent House, I found that it could be brought to Falcon's Nest, the shell of the turtle serving for a basin, as we had long ago proposed. This was an immense convenience.

Thus day succeeded day, and brought its own work: we had no time to be idle nor to lament our separation from our old home in Switzerland, and the society of mankind in general, and of our dear friends in particular. Each of our discoveries or inventions was hailed with delight by the boys; and my wife and I gave frequent thanks to God for so visibly blessing our efforts to make life pleasant in this strange land.

CHAPTER XXIII

The Rainy Season

One morning, while we were busily engaged in adding some finishing touches to our staircase, a strange noise, of a most unwonted character, was heard at a distance. I could form no opinion as to the animal from which the sounds proceeded, and dreaded the attack of some beast of prey.

We at once proceeded to prepare for a vigorous defence. Hurriedly assembling the cattle under the tree, we mounted to our castle, and stood in anxious and eager expectation, with loaded guns, our dogs close at hand. Suddenly Fritz, casting aside his gun, rushed forward, and, bursting into a loud laugh, exclaimed, 'It is the donkey, papa! Poor old Grizzle!' At this moment the sound was repeated close at hand, and excited the utmost mirth amongst us all, as we recognised the unmistakable 'he-haws' of our old and faithful servant, whom we now recaptured with ease.

But he was not alone. Close by his side was a magnificent young onager,* whose hideous braying had first startled us. Without delay I set about capturing the beast, and with much difficulty succeeded in passing a slipknot over his head On feeling the rope tighten he at once started, and, with a backward bound, was turning to fly. But the sudden jerk brought him up, and he fell to the ground as if suffocated, for the rope was choking him.

Loosening the cord, and replacing it by one of our donkey's halters, I securely fastened him with two long ropes to the roots

---

* The onager (*ŏn'-ă-jĕr*), or wild ass, originally inhabited the great deserts of Central Asia, and is still found there in its wild state. It is a handsome animal, and exceedingly sure footed.

of our tree, and left him there till hunger should complete his subjection. IIe, however, made a brave struggle to regain his liberty. Having fettered the forelegs of the ass, I tethered him besides the onager and left them together.

In the course of a few weeks we managed to tame and educate him, and he became so well broken that we were able to mount on his back without fear. Lightfoot, as we called him, then became a most valuable addition to our beasts of burden.

Our stock of animals had by this time become large. Three successive hatchings by our fowls had put us in possession of forty little chickens, which ran about in all directions, to the delight of my wife, who looked upon them as a great accession to our security and comfort.

These additions, together with several other circumstances, all reminded me again of the necessity of contriving a more convenient place of shelter for our animals and feathered-folk before the rainy season commenced, which I knew could not be far distant, and we now set to work to complete a set of stables and offices for our livestock.

I decided upon covering over the arched roots of our tree, and to use the space underneath as a sleeping and roosting place. To do this we interlaced bamboo canes over the arches of the roots, and filled the crevices with moss and clay. By this means we succeeded in making a flat solid roof on which we could safely walk, and around it placed a low railing.

Underneath we divided the space into separate stalls and apartments, and so a poultry-yard, hay and provision lofts, and storerooms were all united under one roof.

Our winter quarters were at last completed, and we had but to stock them with food. Day after day we worked bringing in provisions of all kinds.

In one of our excursions Ernest had brought home with him some long prickly-pointed leaves, which he presented to Frank, telling him they would do to make swords with. Whilst he was playing with them, Fritz said, 'Let me make you a whip before they decay; but you must split the leaves for me before I can braid them.'

Struck by the flexibility of the fibres, I examined them more closely, and, though it was a mere conjecture, told my wife that I thought they must be a plant of the same nature as the well-known New Zealand flax.*

'Oh,' she said, 'what a delightful discovery! It is the best you have ever made. Get me a leaf! I can make stockings, shirts, and all sorts of wearing apparel, if it prove to be flax.'

We could not help smiling at her eager zeal; and I reminded her that, even if it were flax, the leaves were not yet made into linen, nor had we enough for that purpose.

The boys, who rejoiced in such an opportunity of gratifying their mother's wishes, set off at their greatest speed to get a supply, and soon returned, each laden with a bundle of the valuable flax, which they placed before their mother.

'You have done well,' I said, 'in bringing your mother so much work. We must all help her to prepare the flax; but first it must be steeped.'

'Steeped, papa? What is that?'

'Flax steeping or retting,' I replied, 'is performed by air, sun, and water, or at least moisture. The plants must stay in water until the soft parts decay, so that the fibres separate. The decayed parts of the plant are thus removed; and the tough, flexible ones, which do not so soon decay, can be made fit for spinning.'

'Would not Flamingo Marsh be a good place for steeping the flax?' asked my wife.

We all approved of her proposal, and on the following morning the ass was harnessed to the little wagon, and the bundles of flax laid upon it, while Frank and Master Nip rode between on the seat. On arriving, the bundles were laid in the water, with heavy stones to keep them from coming to the surface.

---

* The New Zealand flax is a plant of the lily kind. It grows in great tufts, with sword-shaped leaves, sometimes 6ft long. These the natives of New Zealand use for making baskets, and from the fibres cordage and coarse linen is also made. It is used in England, to a less extent, for the same purpose, chiefly in the Dundee trade.

After a fortnight we spread the flax in the sun to dry, and a single day accomplished this so thoroughly that we were able to take it home in the cart the same evening.

The weather had become variable and the nights chilly; whilst frequent showers, and a sky covered with clouds warned us of the approach of the rainy season. Our great care was now to gather a store of potatoes and manioc or cassava roots, sugar-canes, coconuts, sweet acorns, and all kinds of provisions suitable for ourselves and as fodder for our animals. We missed

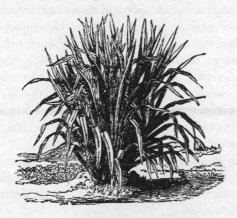

New Zealand flax

more than anything the wheaten flour of which bread is made in our beloved Switzerland; and all the seeds of wheat and other grain that remained in my wife's wonderful bag had been sowed, in the hope that the rainy season would cause them to germinate, and produce an abundant crop by spring.

Before our arrangements were quite completed, the first storm came upon us, and the rain fell in torrents day and night. It was impossible for us to remain in our sleeping apartment, for the rain penetrated in every direction, and we took refuge in the hollow trunk, with whatever provisions we had at hand. Our homely dwelling was so crowded that we could scarcely move, and the smell from the stables, the lowing of the cattle, and the noise made by the fowls, together with the suffocating smoke when we attempted to light a fire, made our situation almost unbearable.

These difficulties were overcome by degrees. The animals were moved further away, and, by piling up articles on the winding staircase, we succeeded in making room enough to work during the day and to lie down at night. Cooking was dispensed with as far as possible, both to spare us the tormenting smoke and to economise our dried wood in case of colder weather.

On the evening of the first day, Fritz and I, in spite of the rain, had to search for the animals, and bring them to shelter under the arched roots; as well as to obtain for them the necessary food. Before I slept I determined to discover some other means of passing the winter, if the weather would enable me to venture out; but no change took place for nearly a week, and during that time we could only subsist on the acorns, coconuts, cold meat, and potatoes that we had brought to our retreat.

We had hay enough for the animals at present, and a stock of grain for the poultry; and I decided that when we were unable to supply them with sufficient food they must be turned adrift to forage for themselves.

A slight change in the weather gladdened my heart, for it enabled me to make some little improvements in our habitation, and with the help of Fritz to bring a store of provisions and fodder from Tent House. The animals being in the spaces under the arched roots, we had the hollow trunk of our tree to ourselves, and by the time the rainy season really set in we were becoming reconciled to our position. Fortunately the winter was not cold as well as wet.

While using our hollow tree as a refuge from the weather, we were still actively employed. Fritz and Jack taught little Francis to read; my wife occupied herself with her needle; while I began a journal of the events which had occurred since the shipwreck, and the story of our lives in this foreign land. This, however, was regarded as a pastime; and my frequent recourse to the memory of the others, with the questions and discussions that arose from it, gave us all great enjoyment. My work, during these dark wintry days, consisted in making coarse and fine carding-combs, and a spindle for the work mother had in prospect, when the weather should make it possible to dry the flax and prepare it for her first experiments in spinning. We also resolved that our first walk, on the return of the fine weather, should be the exploring of the rocks, with a view to the construction of a substantial winter dwelling, before the rainy season set in again.

CHAPTER XXIV

The Salt Cavern

It is impossible to describe our joy when, after three long months of confinement and privation, we again gazed on the clear sky and the bright sunshine. The sorrows of the winter were quite forgotten. No prisoners set at liberty could have felt more joy than we did as we stepped forth from our winter abode, refreshed our eyes with the pleasant verdure around us, and drank in the pure balmy air of spring. We felt ourselves inspired with new hope, and the work which lay before us seemed in our gladness but child's play.

Our tree plantation was in excellent condition. The land we had cultivated was flourishing. The seeds we had sown were springing up, and the trees were putting forth their young leaves of delicate green. The ground was everywhere covered with flowers of varied hues, whose sweet fragrance filled the air; while birds of the most brilliant plumage made the woods resound with song, as if in sympathy with us.

Our first work was at our lodging in the tree. It was sadly dilapidated, for the rain had greatly damaged the sailcloth roof, and twigs and dried leaves had drifted into our sleeping apartment. The stalls of the animals under the arched roots were also damaged, as well as the staircase in the trunk. While Fritz and I were attending to these repairs, Ernest and Jack turned the animals out to graze upon the soft green grass. My wife also reminded me of the flax, which required beating, combing, and carding before it could be spun or woven.

'You will probably find Tent House no less injured by the rain than this,' she added; 'and while you and the older boys are absent I can stay here with little Frank, and spin the flax, for you are sadly in need of clothes.'

The manufacture of a spinning-wheel and reel was by no means an easy task, but by dint of study and perseverance I contrived to turn to account one of the lightest of the wheels I had brought from the wreck, and though rude and clumsy the machines answered the purpose admirably, and my wife was delighted with them. The boys prepared the steeped flax, and we thus had, as she said, all that would be required for a new supply of clothing.

The damage done at Falcon's Nest was but trifling compared to the deplorable destruction at Tent House. The tent was overthrown, the sailcloth covering torn, and so completely soaked were the stores of provisions that the greater part of them would have been destroyed had we not quickly placed them in the sun to dry. Fortunately the pinnace had sustained no injury, although the tub-boat had been knocked about and was now of little value; and two of the three powder-casks were so thoroughly wetted as to be rendered wholly useless.

This latter circumstance led me to study how I might contrive winter quarters where such disasters could not occur; and my mind turned to the bold project of Fritz – to hollow out a cave in the rocks. This was no easy thing with the tools and strength at our disposal, and it seemed impossible, except as the work of several summers. I, however, determined to hew out a place of shelter for our powder stores, and set out one morning with Fritz and Jack to make a beginning of the work.

After carefully examining the whole neighbouring rocks, I selected a part of the cliff which appeared smooth and steep, and from the top of which could be seen a most extended view of Safety Bay and the two banks of the river. Here I marked with charcoal the outline of an opening, and we took upon ourselves the office of stone-delvers.

The work was most exhausting, and our first day's progress was so slight that I despaired of being able to complete even a common cellar before the time of another rainy season. But on the following day we set to work with renewed vigour. The rock under the outer surface became softer, and in a few days more we had penetrated to a distance of about seven feet, when Jack, who was trying to bore a hole with a large crowbar, cried out, 'I am through, papa! I am through!'

'Through what, my boy? Not through your hand, I hope, and you are certainly not through the mountain.'

'Yes, I am, papa! Hurrah, hurrah!'

'Quite right, papa,' said Fritz; 'he is indeed through. The iron spike has gone right into an open space, for I can turn it round as I like.'

Seizing the bar, I worked it about with such force that an opening was soon made large enough for one of the boys to slip through, but, as I approached it, a puff of foul air rushed out, and for a moment I was almost overpowered. 'Come away!' I cried. 'To breathe the air from that opening would be certain death.'

I explained to my boys that, under certain circumstances, foul air, chiefly gas (commonly called carbonic acid gas), accumulates in close caves such as this appeared to be, rendering the air unfit for respiration, and that one of the surest tests of the suitability of air to support life is fire; for a flame will go out in air not fit to breathe. I at once sent them to collect some dry hay, which I lighted and threw into the opening. It was immediately extinguished, even after I several times repeated the experiment; and it was obvious that we must resort to other measures.

We had brought from the wreck a case of fireworks, such as hand-grenades, rockets, and blue lights, intended for signals. I despatched Fritz for some of these, and throw the lighted grenades into the cave. Retiring to a little distance we watched the result. A great explosion, with singular reverberations, followed, and a quantity of the gas rushing out was replaced by pure air. We sent in a few more rockets, which flew around like fiery dragons and ended in a shower of stars and after waiting a little while I again made trial of the lighted grass, which, as it blazed freely, showed that all danger from impure air was removed.

We were yet in ignorance of the depth and dimensions of this unexpected cavern; so I sent our active little Jack to Falcon's Nest, to tell his mother of our joyful discovery and to bring her, and his brothers also, back with him, together with a supply of our wax candles, that we might explore together this wonderful vault.

In about an hour they arrived (during which time Fritz and I enlarged the opening), and we entered the grotto, each bearing a lighted wax-candle. Taking a tinderbox, in case the candles should go out, I led the way, feeling the ground with my feet.

The entrance to the cave

We had not advanced very far, before the appearance of the grotto star led us with its wonderful beauty. The lights that we carried were reflected on the walls in golden light; the columns, which rose from the floor to the vaulted roof, sparkled and glittered with all the colours of the rainbow. Crystals hung from the roof in fantastic forms, and the whole aspect of the place was that of some fairy palace of romance; whilst the floor was covered with soft firm sand, that showed no trace of dampness.

I recalled descriptions I had read of salt-mines in Poland,

and, breaking off a bit of the crystal and putting it to my mouth, I found that we were in a cavern of crystallised rock-salt. Not the least of its advantages would be that both ourselves and our cattle would now be provided with a never-failing supply of this condiment (so necessary to health), instead of the precarious and unsatisfactory one we had hitherto depended upon, viz., that left by the evaporation of the sea water in crevices of the rocks.

Our admiration of the cavern, as we penetrated further, knew no bounds. Plan after plan was quickly proposed for turning it to the best advantage, and our inventive powers were newly excited by this fresh opportunity for their exercise.

It was at last decided that Falcon's Nest should continue to be our summer residence and sleeping quarters, but that the entire day was to be spent at Tent House, while we prepared a winter home at what we now called our Rock Castle.

CHAPTER XXV

A Shoal of Herrings

Nothing was now talked of but the new house, how it should be arranged, and how fitted up. As the inner portion of the rock which we had pierced before reaching our magnificent grotto was soft, and since I anticipated it would harden rapidly on exposure to the air, I resolved to at once make such cuttings as were necessary.

Openings were therefore first hewn out of the rock for admitting light and air, and the doors and windows we had brought from the wreck were transferred from Falcon's Nest and fixed in position. The immense space was then divided into several apartments. At the right of the entrance were to be our dwelling and sleeping rooms, and at the left our kitchen, workshop, and stables. The smaller division, which was so deep in the cave that no windows could be made in it, I determined to use as cellars, storehouses, and magazines. I hoped by degrees to supply the necessary doors, as well as other additions needful for a comfortable dwelling-house; and though our work went slowly on, we laboured with cheerful goodwill to effect the necessary arrangements for adapting it to our use, and did not doubt that it would be sufficiently advanced to enable us to take up our abode in it before winter set in.

Our residence at Tent House, in consequence of our employment, revealed several advantages which we had not foreseen. Turtles frequently came ashore to deposit their eggs in the sand, and from their flesh we had many a sumptuous meal. When more than one appeared at a time, we used to cut off their retreat to the sea, by dexterously turning them on their backs, and then fastening them to a stake driven close to the water's edge by a cord passed through a hole in the shell. We thus had a fresh turtle always within reach, for they throve well, and were in as good condition after several weeks as others freshly caught. But this was not all. A fresh surprise awaited us.

As we approached Tent House one morning we were attracted by a most singular phenomenon. The waters out at sea were curiously agitated, and as they heaved and boiled, struck by the beams of the morning sun, they seemed illuminated by flashes of fire. Over the water where this disturbance was taking place hovered hundreds of birds, screaming loudly, and ever and anon darting downward and plunging beneath the water.

Suddenly this extraordinary mass advanced to the bay, and we found the unusual appearance to be caused by a shoal of herrings* many leagues in extent, and several feet deep.

We lost no time in putting in for a share of the spoil, and soon our fishery was in full operation. Fritz and Jack stood in the water with baskets, and, baling out the fish, threw them on the sand.

My wife and Ernest dressed and rubbed them with salt, and I arranged them in small barrels, a layer of herrings and one of salt alternately. This occupied us several days, at the end of which time a dozen or more barrels of excellent salted provisions were secured against the winter's need. A still larger quantity was slit up and hung on lines under the roof of a small hut of reeds. A fire of green moss and brushwood was then lighted under them which threw out a dense smoke. This smoke effectually preserved or cured the fish, imparting to them, at the same time, a very pleasant flavour.

I also found an empty sailor's chest on the shore, in the sides of which I bored holes, and, putting into it heavy stones, sank it among the rocks. Here it formed a pot for crabs and lobsters, which were drawn by the attractive bait of the refuse of the herrings, and by this contrivance we obtained a constant supply,

---

* The herring is only found in the north temperate regions of the globe. In the early summer the fish leave the deep waters of the ocean for shallower parts, where they can deposit their ova or eggs. They swim near the surface, and are therefore easily caught by net. The herring fishery off the British coast is a most important branch of trade.

the chest being secured by a chain.

Fearing that a change in the weather might come upon us before we expected it, we resumed the work of fitting up our rock-castle. I found, on closer inspection, that the crystallised salt of the cavern had for its base a species of gypsum.*

Breaking off several pieces, and carrying them to Tent House, I heated them red-hot in the fire, and then reduced them to powder. This, when mixed with water, made a beautiful white plaster, which was afterwards of great use to us.

Fortunately, in this beautiful climate, little or no attention was necessary for the kitchen-garden: the seeds sprang up and flourished with apparently not the slightest regard for time or for the season of the year. We had always a succession of delicious fruits and vegetables. Peas, beans, wheat, barley, rye, and maize seemed to be constantly ripening; while cucumbers, melons, pineapples, and all sorts of other vegetables grew luxuriantly. The moisture caused by the heavy rains had no doubt helped to produce this result. I therefore was encouraged to hope that the experiments at Falcon's Nest had proved equally successful; and we started one morning to visit the spot. On our way, we passed the large field in which my wife had sown the European grain, after the potatoes had been taken from the ground.

In one part was barley, in another wheat; and further on we saw rye, peas, millet,† and field-beans in great profusion and luxuriance, all for the most part nearly ready for cutting.

'The harvest has begun already, has it not?' I asked, as an immense flock of birds rose in the air, startled by the dogs, and alarmed by our approach.

Fritz released his eagle, which he always carried hooded and

---

* Gypsum (jĭp'-sŭm), or plaster-of-paris, is a mineral found in various parts of the world, but especially near Paris. It frequently occurs in a crystalline form, and is then known as alabaster. It is chemically a sulphate of lime.

† Millet is the common name of a large number of cereal plants, the grains of which are used for food. It is largely cultivated in the south of Europe, and also in the East Indies, China, Arabia, and Egypt. The leaves and young shoots are used, both green and dried, as fodder for cattle.

perched on his game-bag. The bird had by this time become very tractable, and when Fritz uncovered its eyes, and threw it aloft after one of the fugitives, it seemed to scare the whole flock. Singling out a large quail,* the eagle pounced upon its frightened quarry, and would have made an end of its life in a moment had not Fritz been close at hand to release it from his bird's talons.

The quail

The greater part of this day was spent in securing seed-grain for another year's sowing, and in making preparations for a little excursion which had been proposed for the following day.

---

* The name quail is given to several birds nearly allied to the partridge, and similar to it in general shape, but much smaller. The common quail is a migratory bird, and is found in every country from the North Cape to the Cape of Good Hope. It eats seeds, grain, and small insects, and is an important article of food in the countries it inhabits.

CHAPTER XXVI

Further Work and Discoveries

It was a project of my wife's to establish a kind of farm for our animals at some distance from Falcon's Nest, where they would be secure and would find sustenance for themselves: for they had become too numerous for our limited means to supply them with food. Twelve young fowls, four pigs, and two pair each of sheep and goats, were accordingly spared from our stock for this purpose, and placed in the cart with provisions, and such tools and other utensils as we should need.

Fritz went before to reconnoitre, and we took our way to a part of our domain which had not yet been explored. We had great difficulty, at first, in getting through the high grass, and had frequent recourse to our hatchets, till we reached the opposite end of the wood, where we saw before us an open plain, on which grew numbers of low bushes. They seemed to be covered with snowflakes, if that had been possible, and Fritz presently brought me a branch loaded with beautiful white down, which, to my great joy, I found to be cotton.*

It was a discovery of inestimable value to us, and filled my wife with delight. We gathered all that could be contained in three

---

* The cotton plant – a species of mallow – is found in both the Old and New Worlds, but is cultivated only within the limits of 35° north or south of the Equator. The cotton is a soft downy substance, somewhat resembling fine wool or hair, which surrounds the seeds. The numerous black seeds are contained in a capsule or cup, which succeeds the flowers. When nearly ripe, this capsule bursts open and liberates the cotton, which is then gathered by hand and packed in bales for exportation. During the last 150 years, cotton has become one of our chief manufactures. The principal supply of this raw material for our manufactures, comes from the United States, India, Egypt and Brazil.

capacious bags, and resumed our journey, which took us to the summit of a pretty wooded hill. The view was lovely. Luxuriant grass at our feet stretched down a hillside dotted here and there with shady trees, among which a bright, limpid brook rippled over a rocky bed, while beyond lay the rich verdant forest, with the sea extending to the distant horizon.

What better situation could we hope to find for our new stock-farm? Pasture, water, shade, and shelter, all were here. We accordingly pitched our tent, and at once began the erection of a shed.

The group of trees I had selected for our farmstead stood near together, and formed an oblong, the longest side facing the sea. In the trunks of these, at a suitable distance from the ground, I cut notches, and then, placing beams across, formed a sloping roof and the skeleton of the building.

Having fastened the beams with nails, I covered the roof with pieces of bark, cut in squares, and secured them with the thorns of the acacia,* which we found growing here. Our nails were too precious for lavish use.

With wild vines, reeds, and brushwood, I wove together the outer walls, and in the open space above made trellis work to give a circulation of air and an entrance to light. The interior was divided into two apartments of unequal size – one of which contained the stalls for the cattle and a place shut off with palings for the fowls; and the other sleeping apartments for ourselves, when we should need to pay the place a visit. Above, we made a loft, where fodder could be stored.

As all this took us several days – in fact, longer than we anticipated – our stock of provisions began to fail us. I therefore sent Fritz and Jack to Falcon's Nest to obtain a fresh supply, and

* The acacia ($\check{a}$-$k\bar{a}'$-$sh\bar{e}$-$\check{a}$). There are several plants bearing this name, natives of Arabia, North Africa, and the East Indies. On many of the species a sharp strong thorn grows at the foot of the leaf stalk. One species of acacia (called the Egyptian thorn) produces gum arabic; the bark of another is used in tanning; and several species furnish timber of good quality.

to look after the animals and fowls we had left, and give them
food for ten or twelve days.

They took with them the ass and the onager, to draw the cart
in which to pack our provisions; and during their absence,

The cotton plant

Ernest and myself made an excursion into the neighbourhood to
learn more of the country in the vicinity of our farm. Crossing a
winding stream, we reached a large marsh, where the rice-plant
grew wild in great luxuriance; and a little further on, Master
Nip, who nearly always went with us, made a sudden dart into a
thicket, where I found him regaling himself with strawberries,
that were not only quite ripe but of most delicious aroma and
flavour.

Having refreshed ourselves with them, we filled the basket which Master Nip had been taught to carry on his back (covering it with a thick layer of leaves), lest it should please him to overturn and dispose of his burden. I also pulled some of the rice, that we might ascertain whether it would serve us as food. Continuing our walk, we came presently to a pretty lake, which we had already admired from a distance. On account of the number of swans we saw on its banks, and sailing on its placid waters, we called it Swan Lake.

It was now, however, time to return to the farm, as our messengers might soon arrive; and, sure enough, in about a quarter of an hour after we got back, Fritz and Jack made their appearance, and gave an account of their mission.

I was pleased to see that they had not only carried out all my directions and commissions, but had also brought with them other articles which they judged would be useful in carrying out my plans. We therefore stayed some days longer, completed our new structure, and stored it with a good supply of fodder and grain.

Having provided amply for the animals, we then left the farm (which we had named Wood Grange), on a new excursion that I had long thought about.

Loading our cart, we set off in the direction of Cape Disappointment, and after walking a short distance we reached a wood. Here we were received by an enormous number of apes, who kept up a series of the most unearthly cries, and assailed us with a perfect hailstorm of pine cones, and it was only by firing our guns, loaded with small shot, that we could disperse them.

Fritz picked up one of the cones, and I recognised it as that of the stone pine.*

'Gather some,' I said, 'by all means. You will find that the kernel has a pleasant taste, like that of the almond, and by pressing we can obtain an excellent oil from them.'

* The stone pine grows extensively on the shores of the Mediterranean. The seeds are eatable, and are called pine nuts or pine kernels. They have a sweet taste, somewhat resembling almonds.

After leaving the wood we soon drew near to the Cape. The view from the summit of the little hill was so beautiful that I decided to make another establishment here. Profiting by our experience, the work was far easier to us now, and in six days we had a pretty little rustic abode, to which, at Ernest's suggestion, we gave the name of 'Prospect Hill'.

Much as we had done, the end for which our expedition had been planned was yet unfulfilled, for I had not met with a tree which suited me for making a boat, and which I had specially come in search of.

We returned to the wood for a closer inspection of the trees, and I at last fixed upon a kind of oak, the bark of which was closer than that of the European oak, and more resembled that of the cork tree.* The trunk was at least five feet in diameter, and I fancied that its coating, if I could obtain it whole, would perfectly answer my purpose. I marked a circle at the foot, and with a small saw cut the bark entirely through. Fritz attached the rope ladder, which we had brought with us, to the tree, and sawed a similar circle eighteen feet above mine. We then cut out perpendicularly a slip of the whole length, and, after removing it, had room to insert wedges and other tools for loosening the whole bark. It was a difficult matter, but we succeeded at last, and I began my boat while the material was fresh and flexible.

From each end of the roll of bark I cut a wedge-shaped piece about five feet long, and closed the edges with pegs and strong cement, so that they formed a point at each extremity. Having, by so doing, widened it too much in the middle, we put strong ropes around, and drew it into the form we desired, and left it to dry and harden in the sun. As this was all that I could do without other tools, I despatched Fritz and Jack for the sledge, that the canoe might be transported to the vicinity of Tent House.

* The cork tree is a species of evergreen oak growing in the south of Europe (especially in Spain and Portugal) and the north of Africa. It grows from 20 to 40 feet high, and has a thick rough outer bark. This outer bark is taken off, and forms the article cork. The bark grows again in from six to seven years, and is then fit for use.

During their absence the boat dried into a proper shape, and I cut some naturally curved branches from a tree growing near, just suited for ribs, to support and strengthen the sides. These greatly improved its shape.

When the lads returned, it was time to rest for the night; but with early dawn we were again busily at work, and placing our canoe on the sledge, we loaded it with all that it would hold, and reached Tent House some time before sunset. We were too tired to do anything more that night. With renewed energy, however, we set to work next morning, and the boat was soon ready to be launched.

It was lined with wood and furnished with a keel and seats. Instead of ballast, I laid at the bottom a layer of stones covered with clay, and over this a flooring of boards, whilst in the middle rose a movable bamboo mast with a triangular sail. The stern was neatly fitted with a rudder, and the whole was well pitched outside to make it watertight. When our labours were completed we were delighted with its elegant appearance in the water, and felt that we were now amply provided with means for making marine excursions – the pinnace for distant voyages and the canoe for short excursions along the coast.

CHAPTER XXVII

More Improvements

Whilst this work was in progress we were not unmindful of the necessity for completing our winter residence before the return of the next rainy season.

Much of our time was occupied in reaping, planting, looking after our various colonies of livestock, and in gathering in an abundance of necessary stores; but for two months we worked steadily some part of each day at our grotto, in order to complete it, and to put the rooms and stalls for the animals in comfortable order. During the next long rainy season, when other work would be at a standstill, we intended to carry out many minor details for the embellishment of our abode. We levelled the floors first with clay; then spread gravel mixed with gypsum and water over that, producing a firm and smooth surface like concrete. But I was ambitious to provide some European luxuries as part of our domestic furnishings – amongst other things, to have one or two carpets – and set about making a kind of felt in the following way –

Spreading a large piece of sailcloth on the ground, I saturated it thoroughly with a strong liquid made of gum (the produce of certain trees) and isinglass (which we had manufactured from the sounds of several large species of fish we had captured), and laid upon it wool and hair from the sheep and goats, which had been previously cleaned and prepared. We then rolled up the cloth, and beat it well until the wool and hair compacted together. When dry, our covering for the floor was by no means to be despised, and it formed an effectual protection against damp during the rainy season.

For a considerable time no event of importance occurred. Our work went on with little incident until Jack broke the monotony by presenting himself one morning, after a short absence, in a most deplorable condition, covered from head to foot with thick green mud. A great bundle of canes was on his back, muddy and green like himself. He had lost a shoe, and altogether he presented so ludicrous a picture of misery that we could not help laughing, though he seemed ready to cry.

'My dear boy, what have you been doing?' I asked.

'Gathering reeds,' he replied, 'in the marsh. I wanted to make some cages and baskets, and I saw such beauties on the edge of the marsh that I couldn't help trying to get them. I jumped from one tuft of firm earth to another quite safely, till I got near the reeds, and then my foot slipped, and in I went – first up to my ankles, and then to my knees – and there I stuck, and began to scream with all my might; but no one came to help me. At last, in my terror, I thought of the reeds. I could just reach them with my knife; so I cut down this bundle, and laid it on the edge of the marshy pool, to form a kind of bank, and, while I rested my body upon it, I was able to set my legs free; but I left one of my shoes behind. I never had such a fright in my life as when I felt myself sinking in the marsh. I thought it was all over with me.'

'Thank God for such a fortunate escape, my boy,' I said, 'and also for giving you the courage and presence of mind to act as you did.'

I examined the reeds, and found that I could use them for making parts of a weaving-loom for my wife. By splitting two of the largest I formed a frame for the warp; and the boys cut some of the more slender ones into small pieces for teeth for the comb. Their curiosity was excited, especially as I had each part carefully put away when finished. At last I told them not to be surprised if they found I had made a musical instrument called a 'tam-tam' (a kind of drum such as the natives of the East and West Indies use), which would play a tune when their mother beat time with her foot. They knew I was in fun; but when, at length, the loom was finished and presented to their mother, they quickly understood its value, and watched her movements with intense interest while 'playing the loom', as they always called it.

My next work was to make a turning lathe, which quickly became a special favourite with Ernest, who acquired great dexterity in its use. For several weeks after this was finished we employed ourselves in the interior of our grotto in preparation for winter (for we had come now to the time when any day might mark the beginning of the rainy season), and it became necessary to gather a supply of potatoes, rice, guavas, sweet acorns, pine-cones, and as many of the pineapples as were ripe enough to pluck. A quantity of seeds, both native and European, were also sown in various patches of ground, which we cleared for the purpose.

To preserve the various articles in our storehouse in the rock required a larger number of vessels than we possessed, and I broke up the tub-raft, that we might use the casks for the purpose of storing away our roots and dried fruit.

Winter was at last ushered in by heavy clouds, which spread over the horizon, and were followed by pelting showers. The wind rose to a perfect hurricane, and blew violently from the sea; the waves dashed in foam against the rocks, and frightful storms of thunder and lightning drove us to our shelter in the grotto. It was near the beginning of June, and we had twelve weeks of bad weather before us.

Notwithstanding our previous work in the cave, we still found a great deal to do to render it really comfortable. One great inconvenience arose from want of light. The cave had only four openings – the door, one window for our kitchen, another in the workshop, and one which lighted the sleeping chambers. When the entrance door was closed, the stables and other parts of the cave at the back were in almost total darkness.

To remedy this, I fixed a tall bamboo-cane firmly in the ground (near the centre of the cave), the upper end reaching to the roof. Jack then climbed to the top of it with a pulley and stake, which he fastened to a cleft in the rock. A long string was passed through the pulley, and to it I fastened a lamp which we had brought from the wreck. My dear wife filled it with clear oil, and as it had four wicks it furnished a fair amount of light. By means of the rope and pulley we could place it at a convenient height above our heads, or lower it on to the table.

Now that we could continue our work with ease, Ernest and Frank busied themselves in fitting shelves against the walls of our living room to hold our books; Jack helped his mother to arrange the various culinary utensils on a kind of dresser formed of planks; while Fritz assisted me in fitting up the workshop, and fixing his turning-lathe in its place in one corner. A carpenter's bench stood in the centre, and the tools (with many other useful articles of various kinds) were hung in racks upon the walls.

I was surprised to find what a number of books we had saved from the wreck – voyages and travels, natural histories, various grammars and dictionaries of foreign languages, and many other learned and interesting works. To these were added a box of mathematical and astronomical instruments, several maps and charts, and an excellent globe. Books occupied much of our time, and we all determined to improve our knowledge of English, French, and German during the ten or twelve weeks of our imprisonment and enforced leisure.

By degrees the wind and storm subsided, the rain ceased, the sun appeared, and we were able to venture forth to look once more on nature's smiling aspect of peaceful beauty, and to observe with delight the signs of reviving vegetation.

CHAPTER XXVIII

The Water-Boa

No sooner had the end of the rainy season permitted us to leave the sheltering walls of Rock Castle than I determined to search for a suitable place, near at hand, to be kept expressly for the sowing of our various grains, where they could be properly attended to and reaped in due course. But as our animals were too little accustomed to the yoke to warrant me in attempting to use one of the ploughs I had saved from the wreck, I was obliged to delay the project. I therefore resolved to set aside all fieldwork till just before the next rainy season, and in the meantime fulfil my promise of finishing another weaving machine for my wife, which would enable her to make some substantial fabrics, as our garments had been patched and repaired till they threatened to hang together no longer.

My first efforts had produced but a rough and clumsy loom, which, though it had answered for a time, was now almost useless.

In my young days I had frequently visited the workshops of weavers, and knew something of other trades, which knowledge helped me greatly in our present position. To complete my task I still required the particular paste or weaver's glue with which they cover the warp to prevent it from slipping and tangling, and, in default of it I determined to try fish-glue. I had already contrived to make this gum into sheets, clear and firm enough to be used as windowpanes, and as the windows were placed very deep in the rocky wall (to keep out the rain), they served the purpose admirably, for though not transparent, they admitted the necessary light into our dwelling.

At the repeated request of my boys I had made two saddles and bridles, and a yoke. These I had constructed of light wood, and covered them with the skin of some of the animals we had killed. To stuff them I used the moss of the old trees on which the pigeons built; and the leather for bridles I made soft and flexible by soaking it in oil.

This work occupied a considerable time, during which we were again visited by a shoal of herrings, large numbers of which we caught. These were followed, as formerly, by other fishes, of which we gathered a large number; for although the flesh was too oily to be eaten, we had baited traps with it for crabs, and besides had found the oil, and the air-bladder or sound (from which we made isinglass) most useful to us.

The boys had several times petitioned me to take them on a hunting expedition, and I consented to do so after we had made two large baskets for carrying grain, fruits, or roots, from the field. We accordingly gathered a quantity of rushes (which grew plentifully on the borders of Jackal River), for our first attempt at basket-making.

Our initial efforts were clumsy enough; but we gained experience, and by and by made larger and better ones of the Spanish canes, and these later trials were quite successful.

As I was one day sitting with my wife and Fritz, in the shadow of some trees overlooking Jackal River, watching the gambols of the boys and talking of the improvements I hoped to make, suddenly Fritz exclaimed, 'Papa, what is that in the distance? It looks like a thick cable, and seems to be coming nearer.'

I ran for the large telescope I had saved from the wreck, and, to my horror, saw an enormous serpent rolling towards us on the sand, and raising itself to look around, as if for prey, and advancing straight towards the grotto.

My wife, seeing my alarm, rushed into our cave, and I ordered the younger boys to follow her.

'What is it?' asked Fritz, as we stood together.

'I think it must be a serpent of frightful size,' I replied. 'You had better join your brothers in the house, and get my largest gun in readiness. I will return for you when I see what can be done.'

I went cautiously forward, and became sure that my worst

fears were well grounded. That most dreadful of serpents, the boa-constrictor,* was crossing the bridge at a rapid rate. I rushed back to our cave-dwelling, into which the animals had been hastily conducted, entered quickly and without noise, and barricaded every door and window as strongly as possible.

The young people were in warlike attitude and fully armed. Fritz offered me his gun, and we placed ourselves at the upper windows (openings we had made in the rock at some considerable height, for ventilation, and which were reached from within by steps), from which we could see without being seen.

By this time the huge monster had passed over the bridge, and after a moment's pause, came rolling along in rings, till at length he placed himself just outside our hidden dwelling in the rock.

Ernest, probably from fear, fired his gun; Jack and Frank immediately followed his example, but the shots, although not one of them touched the creature, frightened him, for he began

* The boa-constrictor is an enormous reptile found chiefly in the marshes of Guiana and other parts of tropical America. The name *boa* is the popular name given to all large serpents that kill their prey by entwining themselves round it, and constricting it (that is squeezing it) to death in its folds. The boa is not poisonous, but its mouth is furnished with rows of strong pointed teeth (four above and two below), which makes its bite very severe. Boa constrictors are sometimes from 12 to 20 feet long and water-boas (the largest of the species) from 30 feet upwards. They all possess enormous strength, appetite, swallow, and powers of digestion. In order to procure its food, the boa lies in wait by the side of some river or pool, where animals are likely to come and quench their thirst. With one spring the boa fixes its teeth in the creature's head, and with a rapidity which the eye cannot follow, coils itself round its victim, and by pressure breaks all its bones, and reduces it almost to a shapeless mass. It then commences to swallow the animal whole, an immense flow of saliva assisting in this process. It then lies torpid for several weeks, until the enormous meal is digested, when it again sallies forth in search of prey. Deer, sheep, and smaller animals form its chief victims, but it has been known to attack the buffalo, and even man. There is however, much uncertainty yet as to the size and habits of the various boas. The python of the Old World corresponds to the boa of the New World.

to roll away with great rapidity, and soon disappeared among the reeds in the marsh.

I regretted our failure bitterly. Strictly forbidding the boys to leave the grotto without my permission, we waited for three whole days in fear of our terrible visitor. But we saw no new signs of him, and began to hope that he had left the marsh by a way unknown to us. The half-wild ducks and geese were, however, evidently aware of the presence of an enemy, and seemed to be in constant agitation, giving proof that the creature was, without doubt, still lurking in the thicket of rushes (which they were accustomed to make their nightly resting place), and might at any moment attack us or the animals, if we ventured to leave the cave. My anxiety and embarrassment increased daily.

We were at last relieved, though not without sad and distressing loss. As completely as Rome was saved by the time-honoured geese of the Capitol,* our garrison was now saved from this critical situation by the ass, our useful old Grizzle.

Our position was rendered the more painful from having no stock of provisions for ourselves, or fodder for the animals; and the hay falling short on the third day, I determined, in this dilemma, to set all the animals at liberty, except the cow, to find food for themselves, by sending them across the river at the ford in charge of Fritz.

* The reference here is to a legend related by the Roman historian Livy. The Gauls of Western Europe had crossed the Alps and taken possession of Northern Italy. They then marched on to Rome (390 BC), and a great battle was fought outside the city, the greater number of the Romans being killed. The Gauls then entered Rome, and massacred the senators as they sat in the vestibules of their houses, and all the other inhabitants except those who had fled to the Capitol for safety. The Capitol was a fortress and temple built on the smallest of the seven hills of Rome. In the dead of night the Gauls climbed up the hill and the foremost of them had just reached the top, when the cackling of some geese (which were kept in the Temple of Juno, close by) roused the sentinels and the dogs, and awoke Marcus Manlius, the consul. He hastily collected a body of men, and succeeded in driving away the enemy. The Gauls were afterwards so completely destroyed, that not one was left to carry home the news of their defeat.

I stood at the entrance of the cave, giving him my last injunctions, while my wife, who was entreating us to be cautious, opened the door, and old Grizzle, who had been shut up and well fed for three days, rushed from his stall, and, before we could stop him, galloped away towards Flamingo Marsh. Our eyes followed him, and in vain we called him by name. To our

The death of the ass

horror we saw the serpent raise his head from the rushes and dart forth. Instantly the poor beast was enclosed in the folds of the monstrous reptile and crushed to death.

'Shoot him, papa! shoot him!' screamed the boys. 'Do save poor Grizzle!'

'It is impossible to save him now, my boys, and firing would only irritate the creature,' I said, 'and perhaps draw him on to attack us. It will soon be over; and while the monster sleeps, as he will after his meal, I will do my best to destroy him.'

'Will he swallow his prey whole?' asked Fritz, as we turned away from the painful sight.

'These serpents have several rows of strong teeth,' I replied, 'which enable them to seize their prey. They then crush it to death with the folds of their body. Even the bones are broken by this pressure, and I believe they lick their prey all over* with the tongue, covering it with a peculiar saliva, which makes it easy to swallow.'

I allowed a few hours to pass before attempting to interfere with our terrible enemy, then, accompanied by Fritz, I directed my steps to the borders of the marsh. Jack followed cautiously behind, and Ernest kept us in sight, though further away.

When at a distance of eighteen or twenty paces both Fritz and I took deliberate aim and fired. The shots seemed to take effect, for the upper half of the body and the jaws remained immovable, though the serpent still glared on us with flashing eyes of impotent rage. But the lower part of the body writhed as if in agony, and the tail moved convulsively striking out blindly in all directions. Two pistol-shots, however, finished the matter, and our joyful shouts of victory called all the family to us.

'I am glad the monster is dead,' said Jack.

'Can we eat serpents?' asked Frank.

'No, no,' replied his mother. 'The flesh of a snake is poisonous.'

'Not always,' I remarked. 'Except the head, (which in some species contains the poison fangs), the flesh is frequently eaten, I believe. And I have also heard that pigs can eat the poisonous rattlesnake† without being injured. I once read that on Lake

---

* This statement is rather doubtful.

† The rattlesnake, which is a native of the warm parts of America, is the most venomous and deadly of this species of serpent. It is especially distinguished by its tail, which ends in a number of horny rings, so jointed together that when the tail is moved, they produce a rattling noise something like that made by crumpling a piece of parchment or thick stiff paper. It is believed a new ring is added each year, when the creature casts its skin. Its mouth is furnished with two sharp poison fangs, through which a deadly poison is pressed when the

THE SWISS FAMILY ROBINSON 155

Superior, one of the large lakes of North America, there was a pretty little island, on which no human beings could dwell, on account of the immense number of rattlesnakes with which it was infested. It happened that a vessel, with a large cargo of living pigs on board, was wrecked near the island. The crew contrived to reach the shore, and land themselves and their cargo; but it was impossible for them to remain, and as soon as the storm ceased they repaired one of the ship's boats, and leaving the pigs to their fate, made their escape with all speed. The forsaken animals dispersed themselves on the island, and in time their owner, coming with another ship, found, to his astonishment, that the pigs were in good condition, fat, and well fed. They had eaten up the rattlesnakes, and the island was, from that time, completely cleared of these venomous creatures.'

'How can we tell the difference between the poisonous and the harmless serpents?' asked Fritz.

'Chiefly by the fangs,' I said, 'which they protrude when alarmed or in danger. The creature rears his body to a great height, opens the glowing, red, upper jaw so frightfully that the lower remains fixed, and displays two threatening fangs, which at other times lie folded back and concealed at the sides of the upper jaw. These fangs are hollow, but so hard that they can easily penetrate the thick leather of a boot. And it is under these that the little bag lies which contains the poison. A tiny drop, which is pressed out while the creature is using the fang, enters the wound, and quickly spreads through the veins and over the entire system, speedily causing death. But we have talked long enough, boys, and must not leave our dead enemy till the morning, for the birds of prey, which are already hovering near, will be only too glad to spoil the skin, which I should like to stuff.' I therefore decided that we would have dinner, and then proceed with our melancholy task.

---

snake seizes its prey. Small animals (as hares, monkeys, &c.) and birds form its food. Its greatest length is from 7 to 8 feet. Both hogs and peccaries (see p. 161) can eat this snake with impunity.

Our first work was to recover the mangled remains of the ass, which, being effected, were then buried in the soft, marshy ground close by. We next yoked the cow to the serpent, and dragged it to a convenient distance from Rock Castle. The process of skinning, stuffing, and sewing up again, took us several days, and was a source of great interest and delight to the boys. When this work was completed, the stuffed creature was neatly wound round a long pole in coils, the head, with the jaws wide open, being arranged to look as formidable as possible.

Ernest had already accumulated sundry stuffed animals, shells, pebbles, corals, and other natural curiosities. This he called his museum, and here the serpent was placed erect, a memento of our escape from a great danger. It was so natural and lifelike that the dogs never passed it without growling. The boys attached a label to the mouth, on which was written –

No Asses Admitted Here

and the double meaning in these words was a jest that pleased us all immensely.

CHAPTER XXIX

Another Excursion

Although the danger to which we had been exposed by the appearance of the serpent was over, I could not rest satisfied until I had searched the island, to learn whether any other of these creatures were to be found upon it.

This resulted in two excursions – one to the marsh and duck-pond, the other to the country about Falcon's Nest. Jack and Ernest both hesitated to accompany me, and expressed a strong desire to remain at the grotto; but I reasoned with them on the folly of becoming slaves to an imaginary terror, and overcame their fears, for I wished my boys to be brave and courageous in times of danger. I thus made them see how much safer and more at ease we should feel after exploring the region and finding no trace of these creatures.

We started together, carrying, in addition to our firearms, some bamboo-canes for staves, and a couple of broad planks for crossing the marsh.

Amongst the crushed reeds and rushes we found many traces of the boa, but no signs either of young ones or eggs. Returning by the edge of the rocks, after a strict search, we came upon another grotto or cave, just where they joined the marsh, and from it flowed a little stream of clear sparkling water. Fritz and myself stepped in on a broad path, beside the stream, and found that the ceiling or vaulted roof was formed of glittering stalactites.* The floor was covered with fine earth, as white as snow,

---

* Stalactites are masses of limy substance, shaped like icicles, found hanging from the roofs of caves. They are formed by the dripping of water containing carbonate of lime. The water evaporates and leaves the chalky matter behind, and thus the stalictite slowly increases in size. When the water drops on to the floor its evaporation there produces a stalagmite.

and I found, to my great satisfaction, after examination, that it was fuller's earth.

'This is a pleasant discovery, and will be of great use in washing our clothes,' I said. 'It is a kind of clay largely used by fullers or cloth-dressers, to cleanse wool (both before and after it is woven) from the grease contained in it, and for this purpose it is much better than any artificial soap.'

The stream grew narrower as we advanced, and I found that it issued from a fissure in the rock at the back of the cave. As the stones about this point were soft, it was easy to remove them and make an opening.

Fritz produced his tinderbox,* and a couple of candles were quickly lighted and stuck on our bamboo-canes. By their clear burning I knew that the air was pure enough to allow us to enter. Leaving Ernest and Jack outside, we crept through the hole, and found ourselves in a large lofty hall with a vaulted roof.

'Oh, papa!' exclaimed Fritz joyfully, 'here is another salt cavern. Look at the crystals.'

'They cannot be salt,' I replied, 'or the water of the brook would taste of it. I am rather of the opinion that this is a cave of rock crystals.'†

'Rock crystals, papa!' exclaimed the boy. 'Then we have made a valuable discovery.'

'Not more valuable here,' I replied, 'than was the bag of gold found by Robinson Crusoe to him.'

Our candles were now nearly burnt out, so we hastened to return to the outer grotto, after having fired a pistol to observe its effect on the crystals. On reaching the outside, Jack startled

---

* Tinder is a substance that easily takes fire, and is made from half-burnt linen rags. It was formerly used (before matches came into general use, about 1834) for obtaining a light, by striking a spark among it by means of a flint and steel. A tinderbox is a little metal box (containing the flint, steel, and tinder) of a convenient size for carrying about in the pocket, &c.

† Rock-crystal is crystallised quartz, often transparent and colourless. It is frequently, but incorrectly, called spar.

me by throwing himself into my arms, sobbing and laughing together, as he exclaimed, 'Oh, papa, I'm so glad you have come! I heard a noise like thunder, and thought the cave had fallen in and crushed you both.'

'It was only the report of my pistol, my dear boy. But why did not Ernest remain with you?'

'Oh, he's gone to that bed of rushes, and probably did not hear the noise.'

I went with haste to look for the boy, and found him busy among the reeds, plaiting a kind of basket with rushes.

'Where are the fish for the basket you are making?' I asked.

'I've not been fishing,' he answered; 'but I've killed a young boa, I think. There he is, near my gun.'

This rather alarmed me, for I knew that if this was a young serpent there would probably be more on the marsh. A single glance relieved me. 'Your boa,' I said, 'is a fine fat eel, which will provide us an excellent supper; and we may as well go home now, and show your mother the magnificent fish you have killed.'

I proposed next day that the whole family should accompany me in an excursion to the further side of the Great Bay.

Joyful preparations began at once, and occupied us for nearly a week. The cart was stocked with provisions for an absence of some length, together with our canvas tent, cooking utensils, tools, candles, and plenty of arms and ammunition; and thus equipped we started.

Traces of the boa were occasionally seen, but before we reached Falcon's Nest they had completely disappeared.

We found the livestock in good condition, and their numbers had increased; so after throwing some fodder and salt to them, we then pushed on to Wood Grange. I decided to make this our halting-place for the night, and after a slight dinner we set out to explore the vicinity. Little Frank accompanied us, armed for the first time with a small gun. I took to the left of Black Swan Lake, with Frank; Jack and Fritz took the opposite direction; and Ernest remained to assist his mother in gathering rice from the marshy fens by the lake.

We kept, for the most part, close to the shore; and started many aquatic birds, such as herons, woodcocks, and wild ducks, that flew to the lake, either to sport on its surface or soar above it. After a time, as we met with no adventure (except that Frank shot a little animal called a cavy,* which startled us by rushing from among the reeds), we turned our steps homeward to the tent, having made no discovery of importance.

'And what have you been doing during my absence, Ernest?'

'Oh,' replied he, 'while mamma and I were gathering rice, I noticed several little mounds, like molehills, rising a few inches above the ground. Presently Master Nip, venturing near, drew from a hole in one of them a large rat. I ran to help him, and, after killing the rat, poked my stick into the nest, when out rushed a large number of rats, and escaped among the rice.

'I knocked over some of them with my stick; but their cries brought a whole colony upon me, and they began to attack my legs most savagely. I killed several, but they were so furious that I cried out for help. Juno then dashed in among my assailants, and with one grip of the neck laid many of them dead, and put the rest to flight.'

I was very curious to see the nests, which I found to be similar to those of the beaver. 'They are evidently muskrats,'† I said. 'They resemble the beaver in the cleverness with which they build their houses, and in having a bushy tail and webbed feet.'

---

* The cavy or guinea-pig is a native of tropical America. It is about seven inches long, and of a white colour, variegated with spots of orange and black. There are several species. The agouti belongs to the cavy family. The name 'guinea-pig' is a great mistake, as the animal has nothing to do with Guinea, being only found native in South America. Perhaps guinea is a corruption of Guiana, and pig may have been suggested by the shape of the hind quarters, and the absence of a tail, as in the peccaries.

† The muskrat is a little animal, about the size of a small rabbit, found in North America. In its appearance and habits it resembles the beaver. It is hunted for its skin, which was formerly used in the manufacture of hats. The peculiar smell of musk, which distinguishes it, is not perceived in winter. Its popular name in America is musquash.

Jack and Fritz had by this time returned. They had seen nothing of our dreaded foe, and like ourselves had met with no adventures. They opened their game bags, and produced several wild fruits of various kinds, which we all enjoyed.

It was now growing late, and the boys all looked weary: we therefore took up our night-quarters in the hut or arbour at Wood Grange.

After an early breakfast we continued our journey to the sugar-cane grove. I was thankful to observe no traces of the serpent's trail, and we were proceeding to explore the canebrake, when what appeared to be a herd of little grey-coloured pigs passed before us. The perfect order in which they followed their leader was most remarkable. With a shot from my double-barrelled gun I brought two of them to the ground.

Strange to say, the procession did not pause, but actually passed the dead bodies of their comrades with steady steps, and without breaking rank. Fritz and Jack fired also; and altogether we shot about a dozen of them.

On examining our booty, I recognised they were the peccary,* and as the flesh is considered palatable, Fritz and I at once carefully removed the musk-bag from each, without breaking it. By doing this the flesh was preserved from having a very disagreeable flavour imparted to it.

The peccary

I sent Jack for the cart, and on his arrival we placed the little pigs upon

---

* The peccary is an animal similar to the hog, found in most parts of South America. It feeds chiefly on acorns, roots, and fruits, as well as on worms and small insects. There is no tail, but under the loins is a glandular opening, which secretes a fetid humour (a kind of musk), which must be cut out immediately the animal is killed, or the whole flesh is spoilt for eating. The common peccary is about the size of a small pig, and the flesh is much like pork in appearance and flavour. The peccary is sometimes called the musk-pig.

it, and returned to the arbour, beginning, after a hasty but substantial meal, the preparation of this new supply of provisions. The legs and sides were cut off and salted, and on the day following the boys arranged to turn our arbour into a smoke-house, like the one we used for smoking herrings, and in this the salted joints were hung.

As the smoke in the hut required attention for a few days before the hams would be cured, my wife and one of the boys decided to remain near and attend to the fire, while the rest of us made excursions in the neighbourhood.

On our way to Prospect Hill one morning, we passed through Wood Grange, and I found, to my dismay and mortification, that some wild animals had again attacked the farm buildings. The goats and sheep had wandered away, the fowls also had disappeared, and the stalls and poultry-houses were broken and destroyed. It was therefore obvious that our plans for preserving and multiplying our stock by this means was a complete failure.

CHAPTER XXX

Adventures in a New Country

We now resolved on a more extended survey, and early one morning our caravan set out. After walking several hours, we reached the outskirts of a small wood.

The spot was tolerably cool and well sheltered. On the right was an overhanging rock, while at the left a river emptied itself into a large bay. The place appeared to be safe and convenient, and we began the necessary arrangements for a prolonged stay.

I decided to take the three elder boys with me next day, in order that we might explore the broad plain, or savanna, which we had seen on a former occasion from Prospect Hill. My wife and Frank were to remain at the tent, with the wagons and the animals.

Starting for the unknown land, and taking the narrow pass between the river and the rocks, we arrived at a spot from which the entire plain could be seen spread out before us. Beyond it rose steep barren mountains, piled one above the other, their summits reaching to the clouds, or sharply defined against the sky.

Leaving the verdant plain behind us, and continuing towards the mountain range, we found the contrast increasingly perceptible. The grass was burned, and the land appeared dry and unfruitful; the soil, evidently rocky and sterile, required frequent rain to soften it so as to produce vegetation.

On we walked. The air was sultry and most oppressive, and my poor boys seemed to lose all courage and power of endurance.

At last, when quite overcome with heat and fatigue, we reached the foot of a projecting rock, and threw ourselves down to rest in its grateful and acceptable shade.

We had not been resting long, and had just produced our

provisions, when Fritz, who had his eyes fixed on something in the distance, exclaimed,

'Papa, what is that in the valley yonder? It appears like a man on horseback. And there is another, and a third,' he added; 'and now they are all in full gallop. Can they really be the Arabs of the desert?'

'No, certainly not,' I replied with a laugh. 'But take my telescope, and make out exactly what the strange sight is.'

'It is most curious, papa,' said the boy. 'The moving objects look like herds of cattle, loaded wagons, or wandering haystacks. What can it all be?' The glass was passed to his brothers, and both Ernest and Jack declared the great moving objects to be men on horseback.

I took the telescope myself, and discovered at a glance that the figures were gigantic ostriches.*

The birds were evidently approaching us. I desired Fritz and Jack to call in the dogs, and search for the monkey, while Ernest and myself concealed ourselves. Master Nip, it appeared, had scented water, and the party had refreshed themselves with a hasty bath and filled their water-flasks.

All this time the ostriches were drawing nearer. There were five of them, and one I saw was a male bird, as was shown by the large and beautiful tail feathers, and the deep glossy black of the neck and body.

* The ostrich is the largest of known birds, and is distinguished for its great size and beautiful plumage, especially the male bird. The head is small, and the neck and legs long. The feet have only two toes, and the wings are too short to be used for flight, but are useful to aid in running. The wings and tail have long, soft, drooping plumes. The true ostrich is a native of the sandy deserts of Africa and Arabia. The South American ostrich is quite a different kind of bird. Ostriches can run with extraordinary speed, outdistancing the fleetest horse. Their food consists of grass, grain, and other vegetable substances. The eggs are of great size, averaging 3lb each (about equal to two dozen hen's eggs). Each female is supposed to lay about ten eggs, and several hens lay in the same nest, which is merely a hole scraped in the sand. The eggs appear to be hatched by the parent birds sitting on them in turns and partly by the heat of the sun.

'We must not startle them,' I said, 'lest they begin to run.'

'How do the Arabs catch them?' asked Jack.

'Sometimes on horseback, but oftener by stratagem. When it finds itself pursued, the ostrich will run for hours in a circle of immense circumference, and the hunter keeps within the circle, but still follows, till the creature flags from fatigue, then, crossing the circle, he makes the capture. But, hush! do not move. The birds are very near us.'

The ostrich hunt

Coming upon us so suddenly, they appeared to be startled; and, unfortunately, the impatient dogs escaped from our hold, and rushed, yelping and barking, upon them. Away they flew like the wind, seeming scarcely to touch the ground with their feet. Fritz had uncovered the eyes of his eagle when the birds were first alarmed, and it quickly pounced upon the beautiful male bird, which was a little in the rear, and with one blow of his beak brought the creature to the ground. We were too late to save its life, for the dogs were quickly upon it, and we arrived at the spot only in time to gather up a few of the most beautiful feathers.

'What a pity to kill such a beautiful creature!' said Fritz. 'Why, he must be six feet high, at least, and his neck would measure three feet more.'

'What can these birds find to live upon in this barren and unfruitful spot?' said Ernest.

'It is said that the ostrich can digest almost anything,' I replied; 'but his usual food consists of grains, plants, and shrubs. Most animals, also, that inhabit the barren regions of a desert can live for days without food.'

Continuing our walk towards a valley, which I had seen in the distance, Ernest and Jack turned aside to follow the movements of the dogs. All at once they stood still by some withered shrubs, and beckoned excitely to us to follow.

'Ostrich's eggs! ostrich's eggs!' cried the boys, as we overtook them; and at their feet, in a hole in the sand, exposed to the sun, lay twenty eggs as large as a young child's head.

'That is a glorious discovery!' I said; 'but do not disturb the eggs, or perhaps the mother will forsake them, for she only leaves her eggs during the day; at night she sits on them, covering them carefully.'

The boys begged me to let them take home two eggs, to show to their mother. I cautiously lifted two from the top, and then set up in the sand a cross made of two pieces of the heath-stem, by which to find the nest easily when we should coma again. Turning our steps homewards, where a glad welcome awaited us, we arrived just about sunset at the tent.

CHAPTER XXXI

Another Ostrich Hunt

Next morning I aroused my children early, as I intended that there should be at least one more excursion before returning to Rock House, where many arrangements had to be made in preparation for the approaching rainy season; and I wished especially to discover whether the ostrich had deserted the eggs we had left in the sand. Ernest wished to remain at home to help his mother; for the quiet, indolent boy took very little interest in these fatiguing excursions. Frank gladly joined the elder boys: he was a spirited little fellow, and as fond of enterprise as Jack.

We set out with the cow and the onager and the two old dogs. Taking the direction we had followed on our first visit to Wood Grange, we arrived shortly at the rising ground from which we had seen the ostriches.

I allowed Jack and Frank to gallop forward at full speed over the plain, on condition that they should not allow me to lose sight of them, while Fritz and I quickly followed. When we had nearly reached the ostrich's nest, I observed in the distance four magnificent birds approaching us with almost incredible swiftness. They were close within gunshot before they perceived us, and Fritz sent up his eagle, which at once pounced upon the head of the nearest ostrich. In consequence of his beak being firmly bound up, he could only beat his wings on the creature's back without hurting him.

This, however, so confused and alarmed the bird that he could not defend himself, nor continue his flight. Jack quickly threw the lasso, but instead of catching only the legs, as he intended, he entangled the string also in the wings. The bird fell to the ground at once, and the boys set up shouts of joy as they ran to the spot. Fritz called off his eagle, and drove away the dogs, while I lost no time in endeavouring to tie the legs and set the wings free. The struggles of the prostrate bird were fearful, and the violence with which he kicked right and left with his entangled legs made us fear to approach him. I had begun to despair of making him a prisoner, when happily I thought of covering his eyes by throwing my hunting-pouch over his head. We had no further trouble. All resistance ceased; he lay still as a lamb, and I was able to fasten about his body a broad strip of hide, and on each side of this to attach a piece of strong cord, that we might lead him. I also tied the two legs together with a cord of sufficient length to allow him to walk, but not to make his escape.

'You remember having read of the manner in which the natives of Ceylon secure the newly-captured elephants?' I said to the boys.

'Oh, yes!' answered Fritz. 'They tie the wild animal between two tame elephants, and so it is obliged to obey whether it will or no.'

'Good!' replied Jack, laughing; 'but where are the two tame ostriches to lead this one?'

I replied with a laugh: 'Are you sure they must be ostriches? Have we not our animals?'

'Oh, papa,' cried all the boys, 'that is a famous plan! it is sure not to fail.'

I led the onager and the cow, one on each side of the animal, who still lay on the ground. To the strings which I had fastened to the strip of hide, I attached two leading-reins, one of which I fixed to the bridle of the ass and the other to the horns of the cow. Jack and Frank then mounted and I removed the covering from the bird's eyes. For some moments he remained without moving, as if perplexed and astonished; then, with a sudden spring, rose to his feet, and, seeing no obstacle in his way, darted forward so quickly that the sudden jerk of the reins brought him on his knees. He was soon up again, and began to struggle violently, rushing right and left, in vain attempts to escape; but after a few unavailing struggles he gave way, and sank again to the ground.

After a few minutes' rest the captive rose to his feet, and as the animals at the same moment moved forward he commenced to accommodate himself to their steps, and was completely subdued.

The eagle and the ostrich

Leaving the boys to walk on slowly homewards with their prisoner, Fritz and I proceeded to the spot where we had left the eggs of the ostrich. On reaching the place, we found evident signs that the hen-bird had not abandoned her eggs, and it raised joyful hopes in our minds that we might very soon find little ostrich chicks running about.

Selecting a few of the eggs, we left the rest to the mother's care; and after packing our fragile treasures in cotton-wool (in a bag I had brought for the purpose), we started to rejoin the boys and their captive. From thence we at once proceeded homeward through the green valley, and arrived safely at the tent, rather earlier than we were expected.

The admiration expressed by my wife when she saw our gigantic prize was quickly turned to anxiety. 'How do you suppose we are to feed that enormous creature? and where is he to live? I cannot see that he will be of any possible use.'

'Mamma, I will teach him to carry me on his back,' exclaimed Jack. 'And someday, if we find that our island is joined to Africa or South America, I shall be able to get to these places in a few days, and bring back all sorts of news. He flies like the wind, and his name ought to be Hurricane. Do let me learn to ride him, papa.'

As each of the boys wanted the bird, I settled the matter in this way: 'If Jack succeeds in taming the creature,' I said, 'and teaching him to receive a rider on his back, and to answer the movements of the bridle like a horse, then I am sure he will deserve to consider the animal his own, as a reward for his exertions. From this time, therefore, he is responsible for the training of the ostrich.'

It was now late. I therefore untied the leading-reins, and with the assistance of the boys I fastened them around the stems of two trees, between which the ostrich could stand or lie down as he wished, but could not escape.

The rest of the day we employed in packing the many valuable things we had discovered during these excursions, for removal to the summer lodging we had constructed at Tent House.

CHAPTER XXXII

Ostrich Training

We started early next day to proceed on our way and presented a most singular cavalcade. The ostrich was still so untamed, and retarded our progress so much, that we were obliged to fasten him to the cart by the side of Lightfoot.

On arriving with our various acquisitions at Rock Castle, my wife's first care was to throw open the doors and windows to admit the fresh air. The ostrich was securely tied between two bamboo canes in front of the dwelling, and during the day I relaxed the cords sufficiently to allow it as much freedom of movement as was consistent with its safety. Here I determined it should remain until it became quite tame and tractable.

Our next care was to look after the ostrich eggs. Those which we fancied contained young birds were wrapped in wool. I then constructed a drying-oven, to be kept at a proper temperature as shown by a thermometer, in the hope that they might be hatched by artificial heat, in the way that the Egyptians are accustomed to do with the eggs of their poultry. Four young birds were ultimately hatched, but they all died in a few days after.

These arrangements employed us two days; and now several duties presented themselves, all apparently of equal importance – the cultivation of a piece of land to receive wheat, barley, and maize, and another piece for rice; the taming of the ostrich; and the preparation of the skins of the animals we had captured in our last expedition.

We decided that agricultural work was the most important; and the animals being now accustomed to the yoke were made useful in drawing the plough. But the ploughshare was a light one, and did not turn up the earth deep enough. We had, consequently, to dig, hoe, and work with all our strength. It was not possible to follow this laborious employment during the heat of the day. We therefore worked for two hours in the early morning, and another two in the cool of the evening.

During the intervals of rest I undertook the training of our new captive, the ostrich, but with little success, for it appeared untamable. I was therefore compelled to use the means adopted in taming the eagle, and stupefy the poor creature with the fumes of tobacco.

The powerful effect it had rather alarmed me, for the bird fell to the earth, and remained for some time motionless. When at last it raised its head I lengthened the string, that it might get up and walk around the bamboo-canes to which it was tied. My wife then brought all kinds of nourishment which she thought the creature would eat; but although subdued it refused everything that was offered it for three whole days, and became so feeble and weak that we feared it would die.

As a last resort she made balls of crushed maize mixed with butter, one of which she placed inside its beak. It was immediately swallowed with ease. A second and a third were eagerly looked for, and from that moment its appetite returned, it ate whatever was offered it, soon recovered its strength, and we began to doubt whether we should find enough to feed it. The boys were surprised one day to find the creature swallowing small pebbles; but I explained that the ostrich requires these to enable it to digest its food, just as small birds need gravel.

Whirlwind, as Jack had named it, lived principally on vegetables, maize, and acorns, and at last became so tame that we could do as we liked with it. In less than a month it had been trained by Jack to walk and run with the boy on his back so cleverly, and to sit down, get up, and gallop at command, that I began to consider to what extent we might make it useful as a riding-horse.

I could easily contrive a saddle; but how could a bit be made to suit a bird's beak, or reins to guide an ostrich? In my embarrassment I was almost inclined to give it up, when I recollected that the change from light to darkness, or the contrary, had great influence over the creature, and I conceived the idea of making a leathern hood, somewhat like the one worn by Fritz's eagle. It was to reach from the back of the head to the commencement of the beak in front, and to have holes cut in it for the eyes and ears. Having fitted this to the bird's head, I fastened a ring on each side, and my wife sewed on strings for tying it under its throat.

Over the eyeholes two square flaps were sewed, like the blinkers of a horse's bridle, to be raised or let fall by straps connected with the reins, which were fastened at each end to the rings at the beak. I hoped by this arrangement to guide our feathered courser, for if the rider wished to go straight forward both eyeholes would remain uncovered; to make the creature turn to the left the blinker over the right eye must be shut, or if to the right, the left eye must be covered. To stop the bird the light must be shut out from both eyes.

The performance proved more difficult to carry out than I had expected; but by degrees the tormented animal submitted, and appeared to understand in a very short time the meaning of the covered or uncovered eyes, and to obey the movement of the bridle.

The saddle was placed near the neck of the ostrich, partly resting on the shoulders and partly on the back, being fastened by a girth under the wings and across the breast. This position was necessary, as the slope of the back would have rendered it unsafe; and the shoulders are the strongest part of a bird's back.

We did not expect Master Whirlwind to act as a beast of burden, but as a fleet courser, and, with Jack as its rider, its journeys between Falcon's Nest and Rock Castle were performed with astonishing rapidity.

While busy with this and other useful employments, the rainy season began once more. The first few weeks passed very pleasantly; but notwithstanding various industrial occupations that engaged our attention, such as the daily care of the animals, together with the lessons and daily readings, the time soon began to drag heavily. Fritz at last came to the rescue.

'Now,' said he, 'that we have in the ostrich a rapid traveller by land, might we not contrive something to cut through the sea with equal speed? What if we were to make a kayak,* or Greenlander's canoe?'

This proposition was hailed with enthusiasm by us all, except my dear wife, who always felt anxious when any of us were on the water. I endeavoured to reassure her by explaining that a kayak was a wonderfully safe kind of canoe, covered with the skin of the seal, and very strong, light, and buoyant. She said no more, but gave her assent to our project.

With plenty of material, and time enough to finish the skeleton of the boat before the return of the fine season, we set about the work with eager interest.

Long thick pieces of whalebone formed the sides of the canoe, which were joined at each end for stem and stern, and fitted into a plank underneath for a keel. Split bamboo-canes built up the sides over the whalebone curves; and the keel, which was at least twelve feet long, was strengthened by a band of copper running the whole length, into which I fixed an iron ring for mooring the boat.

The deck was also made of split bamboo-canes, and extended over the whole of the canoe, except at an opening in the middle, in which the rower could sit on a movable seat, and use oars or paddles.

All this occupied us so completely, that the rain passed away, and the sun shone bright and clear, before our canoe was quite ready to be launched. The sides were covered with the skins of young sharks, and in the forepart a mast with a three-cornered sail was fixed. When at length the little skiff was launched on the water, it bounded like a leathern ball, and floated so lightly that it drew only an inch or two of water.

Before Fritz (whom I considered the rightful owner) could be trusted out to sea alone in this fragile boat, his mother tried her

---

* Kayak (pro. *kă'-ăk*) a light fishing boat, used by fishermen in Greenland, made of sealskin, stretched entirely over a slight wooden frame. A hole is pierced in the middle into which the fisher places himself, wrapped in a coat of sealskin, which is then laced close round the hole to keep out the water. The name is sometimes spelt, but improperly, cajack.

ingenuity in making him a swimming-dress. It was like a double sack, with openings for the head, arms, and feet. The material was soaked in a solution of indiarubber, the double portions, or rather the outside and the lining, being closely sewed together around the edges, with just sufficient opening between them to inflate with air like a balloon. The material having been made airtight, and the little opening closed with a cork, the dress would float, and so support the wearer.

At length, one fine morning, it was settled that Fritz should attire himself in his swimming-dress, which he had purposely inflated with air, to prove it. He was welcomed with shouts of laughter, for the dress stuck out before and behind in a most ludicrous manner.

Without seeming to notice the laughter, he marched forward with the greatest gravity, entered the water, and paddled like a duck across the creek to the shore of Shark's Island. With a shout of triumph he turned and swam back to us, and then entering his new canoe he showed us how dexterously he was able to manoeuvre it.

CHAPTER XXXIII

Wanderers from Home

One morning, soon after the incidents just narrated, I discovered, from various allusions, that the boys were meditating an excursion of their own. To this I conceived no reasonable objection could be offered, for an occasional change of occupation was advantageous to all of us. I accordingly expressed my approbation of the project so soon as it was explained to me. At once Fritz ran off to his mother, who was at work in her garden, and begged of her to give him some meat, as he purposed to make pemmican.

'Very good, my dear boy,' replied she; 'but I must first beg of you to tell me what pemmican is.'

He replied that it was a preparation of meat used by North Americans, and was an especial favourite among the fur-traders of Canada, when they go off on trading excursions among the Red Indians. It consists of boar's or goat's flesh, first cooked and then beaten up into a sort of paste, which forms a most substantial nourishment, since a very small portion suffices for a meal; and as it is very portable, it is thus the most convenient food for travellers. Sometimes it is prepared by first drying the meat in the wind and sun, and pounding it up with the fruit of the shad-bush, commonly called the service-berry.

Fritz was obliged to explain to his mother that he had an excursion in view; and after some little coaxing he gained his point, and returned with the needful supply of meat. This the boys set to work to prepare into pemmican. When it was ready I tasted a piece of it to satisfy Fritz, and found it by no means unpalatable.

But these were not the only preparations. Hampers, sacks, small wickerwork cages, and a variety of other utensils were got ready. The old sledge was next brought out and mounted on a pair of cannon-wheels. A small tent also was taken, along with an abundant supply of ammunition and provisions.

At length the morning of departure arrived. On getting up to see them set out, I observed that Jack carried off, very mysteriously, several of our European pigeons, which he had secured in the small wicker baskets I had before observed.

As my wife had declined to join at present in any expedition, and Ernest also intimated his intention of remaining behind, I resolved likewise to stay at home, and employ the time in constructing an apparatus for crushing the sugar-canes, in order to obtain the sugar in some more manageable form than we had heretofore been able to do – a thing which my wife had long desired.

All the preparations of our travellers were meanwhile completed, and a hearty repast partaken of, during which I availed myself of a favourable opportunity for giving them such good counsel as I thought most suited to their present movements. They departed in high spirits, and we watched them till they crossed the bridge and disappeared beyond the wood that lay inland from Falcon's Nest.

I lost no time in setting about my sugar-mill. I constructed three vertical rollers, between which the sugar-canes could be crushed, and to which I adapted some of the wheels originally designed for the intended sugarworks at the new colony for which our ship was bound. This could be set a-going by harnessing our cow to it, so that much personal labour was thereby spared, and we soon had a most efficient apparatus completed.

While Ernest and I were finding abundant and agreeable occupation in thus taxing our ingenuity for the general good, and occasionally soliciting the advice or assistance of my dear wife, who was watching our proceedings with lively interest, our young adventurers were pushing their way towards the savannah, and experiencing sundry novel adventures, which they failed not to recount to us on their return.

On the first evening of their absence, after a day laboriously and industriously spent, my dear Elizabeth and I were seated at the entrance of our comfortable and well-furnished grotto at Rock Castle, conversing together. Our conversation naturally turned on the absent members of the family; and while my wife and I were wondering and guessing as to what they might then be doing, Ernest surprised us by saying, 'I think it will not be long before we have news of my brothers.' My wife asked him what he meant by such a remark, and I was surprised when Ernest thus replied: 'Tomorrow morning, my dear parents, I hope to be able to communicate to you the news of where they are, and what they are about.'

'Truly,' said I, somewhat ironically, 'do you purpose to set out on a visit to them, and be your own carrier in bringing back the news?' Ernest made no reply; but his mother, whose anxiety about her boys was too great to admit of her indulging in any jesting on the subject, asked him how he could be so thoughtless as to speak in that manner.

'Not at all,' said Ernest. 'I am indulging in no foolish dream, yet I hope before long to communicate news to you of the absent travellers.'

While we were thus conversing a bird alighted on the dove-cote, and entered. It was already so dark that we could not discern whether it was one of our own pigeons or some strange bird; and as it was long past the usual hour for their retiring to rest, I feared it might be some dangerous intruder; but Ernest at once interposed. 'Shut up the dovecote!' said he, 'Shut it up! What would you say if that bird was the bearer of letters from Europe?'

'You speak,' said I, 'as if that country was actually in our vicinity. I am aware, however, that it is sometimes pleasant, my dear Ernest, to indulge in such daydreams. But let us now to bed, and tomorrow you can give audience to your courier, and tell us the news of the world from which we are shut out.' Thus saying, I wished him good-night, and we withdrew to our couches to enjoy our well-earned repose.

CHAPTER XXXIV

The Letter-Carriers

Next morning Ernest rose much earlier than usual, and just as I was quitting my room I saw him descending from the dovecote. As his mother and I sat down to breakfast he entered, carrying a large sealed packet in his hand, like an official letter, and with an air of mock dignity, making at the same time a profound obeisance, he thus addressed me: 'The postmaster of the sovereign lord of Rock Castle, Falcon's Nest, and the surrounding domains, presents his respectful compliments, and prays you to pardon delay in the delivery of these despatches from Wood Grange, and other parts of your territories, as the post did not arrive till late last night.'

My wife and I laughed at the gravity with which he went through his part, naturally supposing the whole to be only a pleasant jest. I replied, accordingly, in the same vein: 'Well, Mr Postmaster, and what is the news of which you are the bearer from our more distant dominions?' To this Ernest replied by breaking the seal, and reading as follows –

The Governor-General of Novel Land, to the Governor of Rock Castle, Falcon's Nest, Prospect Hill, &c., &c., greeting.

MOST HONOURED AND DEAR GOVERNOR – We learn with displeasure that a force of three men, belonging to your colony, has effected an inroad into our country, to prey upon the product of the chase, and have already committed much havoc among the animals of this province. We also learn that a ferocious pair of jaguars has invaded this department, and caused great destruction to the domestic animals of our colony. We therefore pray you to repress these disorders as speedily as possible, to recall those hunters and spoilers, to provide against the further ravages of wild beasts, and to take the necessary steps for otherwise protecting the domestic animals, and maintaining the legal rights of man. Wishing you all health and prosperity.

Given at Sydney Cove, this twelfth day of the eighth month of the fourth year of our colony. As witness my hand,

PHILIP PHILLIPSON, *Governor*

His reading finished, Ernest gave way to a hearty fit of laughter as he saw the half-credulous looks of curiosity and anxiety with which we listened to this extravagant despatch, and began dancing about so wildly that a small note fell from his waistcoat pocket. I reached forward to snatch it up, but Ernest anticipated me.

As he picked it up he said – 'This is a private letter from Sydney Cove. I pray you let me read it to you. It contains, perhaps, truer and more trustworthy details than that of Governor Phillipson, which appears to speak in exaggerated and ungracious terms of the emissaries despatched from this colony.'

'You speak in enigmas, Ernest,' said I. 'Fritz, perhaps, gave you this letter before he set out. Perhaps he had then discovered the traces of a jaguar on the sand.'

'Not at all, my dear papa,' replied Ernest. 'It is indeed a letter from Fritz, sent home to us from Sydney Cove, as they have named that part of the coast. It was a pigeon-messenger that brought it here last night.'

I congratulated the boy on so happy a thought.

'But let us hear the letter,' exclaimed his mother, alarmed at the mention of jaguars, and already picturing to herself all manner of dangers. I was scarcely less impatient myself, so Ernest accordingly read aloud the following letter –

DEAR PARENTS, AND MY DEAR ERNEST – I write to inform you of our journey and safe arrival at the farm. There we found an enormous jaguar, which had killed two of our lambs, and was devouring the carcass of a sheep. Francis courageously attacked and killed it, and he deserves the whole

honour of the victory. Our dogs assisted with their usual
fidelity and bravery. We have spent the day in preparing the
skin, which, you will find, is a beautiful trophy. Our pemmican
is not very palatable, bat we are happily independent of it. We
are all safe and sound, and unite in sending our best love.

Your affectionate son,

FRITZ

This letter was a source of no little satisfaction both to my wife
and myself, and we again and again congratulated Ernest on the
happy device by which a means of communication had been
opened between us and the wanderers; but he was so full of his
novel duties as postmaster that he could scarcely think of
anything else all day.

At last his diligent watch was rewarded by seeing a pigeon
again enter the dovecote towards evening. We immediately
examined the bird, and found a despatch tied under the wing. It
was signed by our boys, and announced in the most laconic
terms that they had passed a pleasant night, and had captured
some black swans. They concluded by intimating their intention
to be at Prospect Hill on the morrow.

This note reassured us. From other missives which reached us
from time to time, we learned the particulars of the capture of
three young swans,* the old ones having proved too strong and

* The swan is the largest and most graceful of our swimming birds. It belongs to
the goose family, is a native of the northern parts of the old and new worlds, and
is migratory, coming further south in the breeding season. Its plumage is white,
but a black swan is found in Australia, and a black-necked one in the southern
part of South America. Swans feed on the seeds and roots of water plants, and on
fish spawn. The half-domesticated, or common swan, is about five feet in length,
often weighs 30lb, and has been known to live 50 years. Swans swim rapidly:
their flight is powerful and long continued; they live in societies, but in breeding
time they part, and take up their nesting ground at some little distance from each
other. The nest is a large mass of reeds and rushes, near the edge of the water, an
islet being generally preferred. From five or seven eggs are laid of a dull greyish-
white colour. The young ones are called cygnets. The flesh is rather coarse, but
used, in old times, to be considered a dainty.

agile. They also captured a beautiful large species of heron,* and startled a large tapir, which somewhat alarmed them by its immense size. They reached Prospect Hill, and passed a night there, greatly disturbed by the howling of monkeys, and surrounded by abundant tokens of their mischievous and destructive work. Late on the morrow they returned home in high glee at their successful excursion, and no less pleased to see us than we were to welcome them.

As we talked over their adventures I found that the boys had made several new and valuable discoveries in the course of their wanderings. I was delighted to recognise among their trophies the cacao-bean, of which chocolate is made, the yam, and also the banana, which forms so important an article of food in various countries of America, and with a little preparation forms a very good substitute for bread. Fritz had gathered a rather large quantity of the cacao-beans,† and I determined to at once utilise them, but their preparation was a difficult matter, and, indeed, I feared my ignorance would prevent us from availing ourselves of the delightful refreshment of chocolate. Ernest,

---

* The heron is a wading bird, very long-lived, and formerly highly valued as an article of food. The heron family is very numerous and is found in almost all parts of the world. The common heron, which is a migratory bird, visiting the United Kingdom from spring to autumn, is about three feet in length, with legs about 17 inches long. The plumage is usually bluish-grey, and the food chiefly fish. During the breeding season herons congregate in large flocks, and build their nests in high trees, many being sometimes on one tree, but at other times they are generally seen alone.

† The cacao-bean (pro. kă'-kā'-ō) is the fruit of the cacao tree, a native of Mexico, but now cultivated in all parts of the tropics. It is a small tree, from 16ft to 18ft high, and the seeds are the part used for food. They are contained in a large pointed oval pod, from 6in to 10in long. This pod contains much sweet and whitish pulp, and from fifty to one hundred seeds or beans as they are called. When dried and roasted and separated from their husk, or outer covering, the beans form cocoa. Chocolate is prepared by grinding the roasted seeds with sugar, and flavouring substances, and then pressing the paste thus made into cakes. Note. Cocoa must not be confounded with the coconut, which is the produce of quite a different tree – the coconut palm.

however, came to my aid, and detailed from his reading the process needful for our purpose. The kernels of the cacao-bean are deprived of the outer husk by the aid of fire; they are then roasted, and afterwards pounded in a heated mortar. The paste thus prepared is mixed with an equal quantity of sugar, and formed into cakes for use. We found these chocolate cakes delicious.

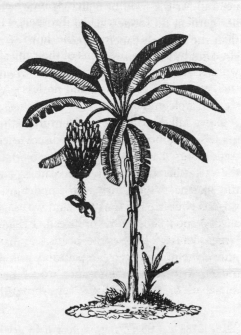

The banana, showing a bunch of fruit

The virtues of the banana* were next discussed, and the boys began to conceive a higher opinion of it when I told them it had been called by travellers the 'king of vegetables', for it

---

* The banana (pro. *bă'-nâ'-nă*) is an East Indian plant, now cultivated in all warm countries. It rises about thirty feet high, and has a tuft of leaves at the top, each leaf being about six feet long and one foot broad. From the leaves and stem of one species a fibre called Manilla hemp is prepared. The flower stem is about four feet long, covered with purple flowers. The fruit is four or five inches long, about an inch in diameter, and grows in large bunches, weighing from sixty to eighty pounds. When ripe they contain much sugar and starch, and are a most nutritious food, being eaten either raw or fried. The young shoots are eaten as vegetables. A greater number of people can live in a given space of ground with the banana than in an equal space of Europe with wheat. From one species of the plant a fine flax is prepared, of which Indian muslin is woven.

includes in its nourishing and palatable properties all that is needful for the food of man. My wife, who was ever mindful of her garden, no sooner heard the praises of the banana set forth than she became eager to have some of the seeds to plant. She also desired to cultivate the cacao-bean where it would be equally accessible, but I told her that the banana was best propagated by slips, and as Ernest assured her that he believed the cacao-beans would not grow unless they were put in very speedily after they were gathered, Fritz went the following morning in his canoe, and brought home the needful supplies for making these valuable additions to our garden.

The yam

He likewise brought back with him several yams.* The fleshy roots (or more properly the tubers) of this most valuable plant are used in the East and West Indies as an article of food, in the same way as potatoes are in more temperate climates. As they are very large, occasionally weighing thirty pounds, he had not room for many of them. We tried to grow them in our garden also (by planting some of the small tubers, which grow at the stem, round the neck of the large tuber), but were not very successful.

* The yam is a native of Africa, and appears to have been imported into India, Malacca, and America. It is now cultivated in most tropical countries. The fleshy roots, or tubers, contain much starch, and generally become somewhat mealy and pleasant to the taste when boiled. It is a climbing plant, and requires to be supported by a pole. The flowers, which are often sweet-scented, and the leaves, are of no use.

CHAPTER XXXV

Conclusion

Chapter has added itself to chapter, as year has added itself to year, and on looking back over what I have written, I cannot avoid wondering what the reader may think of this humble narrative. To me all the minutiae of our daily life were possessed of interest, and I was never weary of recording them; but I must remember it is otherwise with those who may read this story of events – some trivial, some serious – and of the undertakings, small and great, which we have achieved, so I shall pass rapidly over the remaining incidents.

Ten years have passed over our heads, varied only by adventures and occurrences such as those I have already narrated. But these ten years have made a most important difference on my assistants. The younger boys, who, when we landed, were only a source of care and anxiety to their mother and me, had, by that time, grown up to be strong and active youths, more capable even of exertion or fatigue than myself. As they had acquired nearly all their knowledge and habits of life in this strange country (which my wife and I were sometimes tempted to contrast with the remembrances of our native land), their hopes and anticipations were entirely concentrated in our new possessions.

Fritz was now a hardy, vigorous young man of twenty-four years of age. Ernest and Jack had also attained to manhood, and Francis was a lively and active youth of eighteen. They all had fine dispositions, and we had the inestimable advantage of being able to train them up without the risk of any contaminating influences of evil companions, or the temptations of civilised life.

Happiness and contentment reigned throughout our cheerful

colony, and a rich abundance greatly exceeded our utmost wants.

Our various outposts and settlements were no less successful than convenient. Our labours at the Grange and at Prospect Hill were at last crowned with abundant success, and we found it occasionally a pleasant change to remove to the houses we had erected there, and to make them the centre of various expeditions into the country beyond, in which the love of novelty and adventure found abundant gratification.

It almost seemed as if there was nothing left us that we could desire; yet many a look had I cast towards the sea, during the eventful years that intervened since the shipwreck, in the hope of espying a distant sail, and once more greeting other human beings, from whom we had been so long shut out. The same feeling animated me in continuing to store up cotton, spices, ostrich plumes, &c., trusting that someday these things might prove a source of wealth to us, and probably enable us to pay our passage to Europe, or to acquire such additions to our supplies as might become requisite.

My dear wife Elizabeth, and myself, were already feeling the symptoms of approaching age; and, with our own more vivid recollections of the past, it was impossible to preclude some haunting anticipations of the future. We felt (if the place of our settlement was to be our final abode) that some one of us must be destined to be the survivor of all the rest; and to my mind, especially, the thought frequently recurred, with sad forebodings. But these feelings had the blessed result of making me turn my thoughts to heaven, and pray to God that He (who had cared for us amid so many dangers, and surrounded us with so many mercies) would avert from any of us so sad a fate as to perish in solitude, amid scenes which had been the source of so much comfort and happiness.

It is with feelings of a very varied character that I conclude this chapter. God is great, and abundant in goodness and mercy! Such is the reigning sentiment in my heart. But the reader must pardon me if I close this long narrative abruptly and in haste.

It was again drawing towards the close of another rainy season. Already the clouds were beginning to break up. Our first attention was directed to our garden and the plantations in the immediate vicinity of Rock Castle; but as the weather grew more settled we ventured on more distant excursions, and Fritz and Jack set off in the canoe to examine our fort and colony on Shark Island.

Having landed there and found everything in good condition, they proceeded to load and fire the two guns in order to satisfy themselves that both the powder and the cannons remained uninjured from the wet. But what was their surprise, when shortly afterwards they distinctly heard three reports of cannon in the distance! They consulted together, perplexed what to do under the circumstances, but finally decided to hasten home at once and inform me of this strange occurrence.

My attention had been naturally attracted by the report of the guns on Shark Island; but I had heard nothing else. On their assuring me that these had been followed afterwards by three other reports in the distance, my first thought was that they had been deceived by the echo of their own guns. This, however, was an opinion not to be entertained; and what I knew of Fritz's coolness and experience left me no longer any room to doubt the correctness of their conclusions.

How strangely constituted is the human mind! What had been the object of my desires and prayers for many years seemed now an object rather of apprehension and dread than of hope. If there is indeed a ship on our coast, I reasoned with myself, may it not as probably be that of some pirate as one manned by friendly Europeans?

Towards evening the rain, which had only partially subsided, once more commenced to fall with increased violence, and for two days we were entirely confined to the grotto. On the third day, when it began to clear, Jack and Fritz intimated their intention of returning to Shark Island, and trying, by their signals, to ascertain if the stranger was still at hand. To this I agreed, and directed them to get out the canoe, so that I might accompany them. On reaching the fort both guns were fired. But it was now no longer possible to doubt their previous account, for the sound of our guns had scarcely died away in the distance, when we distinctly heard a louder report in the direction of Cape Disappointment, followed at brief intervals by six others. We immediately hastened back to Rock Castle, and informing those at home of what we had heard, we desired them to remain within the grotto, while Fritz and I proceeded in the canoe to reconnoitre.

We coasted along, passing one point after another, without discovering anything, till I began once more to ask myself if the whole might not be an illusion. But it was impossible seriously to entertain this idea. That we had heard the reports of seven guns I could no longer doubt, and the period that had elapsed since the first was heard from Shark Island made it almost certain that the vessel must be at anchor somewhere on the coast.

Suddenly, on rounding a headland, we came full in sight of a fine large European vessel reposing at anchor, and on directing my glass to it I had no difficulty in recognising the English colours flying from its masthead. On satisfying myself that the vessel was really an English ship, I thought it advisable that we should present ourselves to the officers and crew in better trim, and we accordingly returned home as swiftly as we could.

We set to work immediately to get the pinnace in order, and put in a variety of our best fruits (and all the most acceptable supplies we could think of), for carrying as a present to the English ship. Evening set in, notwithstanding our exertions, before these various preparations were completed, and we returned to Rock Castle for the night.

None of us, however, seemed to feel any inclination to sleep; so we sat down together and discussed the use that should be made of this opportunity. My dear wife and I both felt that we were growing old, and that all we needed to render our happiness and the enjoyment of our abundant possessions complete, was the opening up of some communication with Europe. It was altogether different with the young people: they seemed perfectly intoxicated with joy, and with anticipations and indefinite longings for the future.

Next morning we set sail in the pinnace, after an early breakfast. The utmost preparations had been made for giving the most favourable impression on our first appearance, and as soon as we came in sight of the ship we fired off a gun, and then hoisted the English colours.

We were received with all the frank cordiality for which naval officers are noted, and we recounted, as briefly as possible, the history of our shipwreck, and of our sojourn for eleven years on this strange coast.

The remainder of my story must be briefly told. We invited Captain Littleton and his officers to Rock Castle, along with Mr Wolston, an English passenger, who, with his wife and two daughters, had left their native country with a view of settling in one of the British colonies. The latter were so delighted with all they saw at our settlement that it was at length definitely agreed that they should take up their abode permanently with us. Mr Wolston was a wealthy and skilful engineer, and the abundant stores and implements he landed promised to be of no slight advantage to us.

My son Fritz expressed a desire to visit Europe, and it was at length arranged with Captain Littleton that Fritz and Jack should proceed with him to England. Ernest and Frank have no desire to leave us, and already they seem to have formed a lively attachment for the two daughters whom we have received in lieu of those of our family that return to Europe.

We exchanged with the captain some of the productions of the island for gunpowder and other useful stores. The remainder, consisting of furs, spices, fruits, ostrich feathers, &c., were carefully packed and put on board as the fortune of our two sons.

At length the last evening has arrived. I write this on the eve of the departure of my two sons. I have sought once more to impress on them the principles of religion, virtue, and probity, in which they have been reared, and to prepare them as much as possible for once more mingling with the world from which we have been so long shut out For the last time we have all knelt together, while I commended my dear children to the watchful care of their heavenly Father.

We have all passed a nearly sleepless night. As it approaches the hour when we must part with our dear children, the trial seems greater than we had conceived.

Soon after dawn the firing of a cannon announced that the anchor was about to be weighed, and that the voyagers must hasten on board. Fritz takes with him this narrative of our shipwreck and settlement on the desert coast of these once lonely shores. I have charged him to have it published in Europe, being not without hope that it may be useful to others, as furnishing, in some degree, an evidence of the fruits of patience, courage, perseverance, and of Christian submission to the Divine will.

I add these parting lines while the ship's boat is preparing to depart, and I close with my last blessing to my sons. May God Almighty bless them, and keep them. Farewell, my beloved children! Farewell!